Arkansas Heat

VOLUME FOUR

Raising Delgado

By

Karen Marie Coleman

ISBN: 978-1-7328314-9-0

authorkarencoleman@yahoo.com

website: www.karencoleman.org

TABLE OF CONTENTS

CUBAN CARD GAME

Six limousines neatly lined in rows were sitting in the parking lot of a privately owned club. Armed limo drivers assisted their exiting passengers while handing them over to enormously robust Cuban guards, who were also armed with semi-automatic weapons. The guards stood at the entrance, waiting to escort them inside.

It was a beautiful sunny evening in Miami, the first Sunday of the month. This day was set aside for the monthly card games of a group of elderly Cuban ladies who had carried on the tradition for forty-two years. Los Zorros Blancos, or The White Foxes, is comprised of mega-rich women, all with tainted pasts and questionable lives.

They were not socially accepted by other wealthy women their age, and they weren't bothered in the least by not fitting into their elite circles. They considered those women weak and subservient to their rich husbands, blindly being carried on their arms like lap poodles, never really taking control of their own lives. They were mere trophies purchased by wealth, another token to declare a social status that stroked their husbands' egos.

But not these women. They took life by the balls, playing by their own rules and not those of Western society. Each of them brought a piece of their own heritage, as well as secrets from their home country of Cuba, and millions of dollars of ill-gotten gain between them. They sat for hours in privately-owned, smoke-filled clubs, drinking everything from spiked coffee to the strongest of elixirs and eating the finest Cuban cuisine before going to their extreme mansions. On this day, only six of the eight women were in attendance. Two ladies from the group were running late as usual.

Rosalinda Perez was sipping her drink and offering her opinion of their tardiness. She was loud and obnoxious, using profanity-laced words each time she spoke. With her strong, manly facial features, height of six feet, broad shoulders, and masculine personality, she appeared tough and often intimidated others around her.

She was harsh and brash. She often bragged about her influence in the criminal underworld; a real bully, mostly talk and no action. She knew people feared her due to her affiliation with the Delgado cartel and the fact that she stood toe to toe with a low-life drug dealer, killing him during an argument. What others weren't aware of was that her pistol misfired due to a faulty trigger, and she nearly pissed her pants when she realized she'd actually killed the guy. Unlike her counterparts, killing wasn't in her blood.

A few bystanders who'd witnessed the incident bragged of it, and she used the death of her victim to gain the reputation of a badass, but she was nothing more than a loud-mouth coward. She began to speak evil of the two ladies who had yet to arrive. She was known for bashing others when they weren't around but rarely spoke up in their presence. She was tolerated by most of the women in the group because they shared a familiar bond. They'd suffered many hardships in Cuba. They remained a tight-knit bunch vowing to care for each other in America.

The other members were becoming annoyed with her. They tried changing the subject, but she continued her drunken rant for the better part of an hour.

"Forty-two years we've been meeting, no? Where are they? Do Ana and Isabella think they're better than the rest of us? She demands that we be punctual, but she's rarely on time. Is her time too precious to spend with us? Since she's the leader, we should be so grateful that we're allowed in her presence. Shit, sometimes I wish I'd never taken a dime from her. I would've made it without her help. We're supposed to be indebted to her? Continue kissing her ring like that damn Isabella? She walks around like a puppet on a string." With exaggerated arm motions and a mocking tone, she says,

"Ahhh... what can we say about the beautiful Mrs. Isabella Burkett? Everyone loves Queen Isabella with her perfect life. We bask in the glory of her angelic light. We get to gaze upon her loveliness, her beautiful bronze skin, lush silvery hair, her lovely smile, and her toned body, all wrapped up into one tight, neat little bow. Fuck that bitch. I hate her!

And tell me this: Why is it, when Ana loses her sons, our lives are supposed to stop because of it? Hell, I'm glad they're dead because they used to harass my boys. As evil as they were, I'd say someone did us a favor by killing them. Don't get me wrong, I feel bad for her, but to tell you the truth, I'm just about sick of her. Besides, she's losing her edge. She's going soft. I think it's time this group elected a new leader because she's no longer capable of running this syndicate. I think we all know that I'm more qualified for the position."

Marisol Garcia, another one of the ladies, was listening to her complaints. She'd heard enough. She was the youngest of the group, being sixty-two years old. Marisol had been looking forward to this day with her friends. To prepare for her outing, she had a special stylist flown into town for a beauty treatment. The stylist trimmed and curled her short, mahogany hair and finished the look with a complete make-up session. She carefully chose her outfit and was dressed to impress, proudly showing off her new attire. She went all out for the gathering spending thousands of dollars for the trip.

She was there to have a good time, and Rosalinda was souring the mood. She took a sip of her drink while angrily eyeing

Rosalinda and thinking to herself, *"Why doesn't she just shut up already? I really would like to go over and smack her in the mouth."* She remained calm and seated as she was usually non-confrontational. She watched with a furrowed brow as Rosalinda drew in a deep pull from her cigar. She removed the Cohiba from her thin lips with her wrinkled hand that bore deep brown age spots. She exhaled, letting out a blast of smoke, and continued talking. As hard as Marisol tried, she couldn't hold her tongue any longer.

"Rosalinda, you really need to stop speaking of them in that manner. They're our friends; and besides, they're not here to defend themselves. It's not right for you to speak negatively of Ana's deceased children. You don't know what it's like to lose a child, yet you speak so freely on the subject. It's just wrong. Have you forgotten what she's done for you? She didn't have to bring you into this organization. She's helped us all by making us very wealthy, and we owe her our loyalty and gratitude. She started this syndicate. It's her baby. I know she may be hard, but she loves us and has proven it. She could've easily abandoned us long ago, especially you. We constantly have to save you from her wrath. It's your mouth. You talk too damn much, and you're not grateful for anything she's done for you. Sometimes, I wish she'd left you on the streets of Cuba in that rat-hole of a brothel where you were working. You were screwing for pennies while being passed around by drunks and foot soldiers. She cleaned your ass up and brought you into her organization, and you do this to her? Now, I'm not afraid of you, like perhaps some of the others here. I'll speak my mind when I feel it's necessary, and today, my dear Rosalinda, you've gone too far. Put the alcohol away if you can't control yourself. We've all come a long way to be here. We're supposed to be having a great time, but it seems as though you insist on ruining it for the rest of us." Rosalinda angrily retorts,

"Oh shut the fuck up, puta! Who are you to talk? You have your head so far up her ass that you can't see anything but shit. You want to talk tough to me, but you can't speak up for yourself when she's around. You let her walk all over you, and you don't say a word while eating every piece of crap she puts on your plate. Have a seat until you grow some balls, and that goes for the rest of you putas around this table."

As the conversation was taking place, neither of them was aware that the other two ladies had not only come in but had also overheard the entire conversation. Once their presence was made known, an eerie silence overtook the room.

The ladies could tell by the icy stare coming from dark, yet beautiful eyes directed towards Rosalinda that trouble was coming. Fearing the unknown, the women watched as Ana made her way over to the card table.

Stopping just shy of her now enemy, Ana placed her foot on top of Rosalinda's and applied pressure. She leaned in, getting directly into her face. The smell of stale alcohol and cigar smoke on her breath, mixed with an obnoxious odor of perfume, annoyed Ana. She produced a slight frown. With piercing eyes and a rumbling voice, she said,

"Rosalinda, you're one of the most ungrateful bitches on the face of this earth. I've killed for you. I made you rich and gave you my protection. I've even protected your sons and bailed them out of trouble. I've given you access to my best attorneys, judges, and all my contacts. I held nothing back from you. If I had it, I shared it with all of you. I've been more than a friend, and this is how you speak of me? You were being beaten and raped daily in Cuba. No man was willing to pay money to screw you due to your appearance. I fought for you when you were too weak to fight for yourself. I saved you from a life of pain, enslavement, and perhaps an uncertain death, and look where you are today. You were useless to me, but I felt sorry for you in your situation. Since you were a young mother struggling with a young child and pregnant with another, I took you in. You had full-time caregivers for your boys. When they became adults, I gave them a position within my organization. Now you say you want to elect a new leader. You should be the one to take my place? You don't have the spine to do what I do. I've killed thousands, and you've killed what, one? You're worthless, dead weight. You've never done anything to benefit this organization. You're trash and very much the scum that I rescued from Havana. You don't deserve to live. Since you've made yourself my enemy, you will die this day at my hand.... No worries: I won't disgrace my weapon by killing such a lowlife as you. That would be too good for you." Ana turned towards her best friend and said, "Isabella, may I please borrow yours?" Marisol watched as Isabella was getting her weapon. Knowing that Rosalinda was about to die, she slowly stood to her feet and cried out,

"No! Ana, wait!"

Ana knew the woman was about to make another plea for Rosalinda's life, as she'd done many times before. She raised her hand without looking in Marisol's direction. Marisol ceased speaking.

"Marisol, how many times have you pleaded for her life and to no avail? She knows nothing about loyalty to this group, although we've remained loyal to her. She's been this way from the moment we came to America. She's never thanked me for helping her. She always takes and never gives. She's a selfish whore. There's no use in sparing her life."

Marisol looked towards Rosalinda and then shifted her eyes back to Ana.

"Ana, I wasn't about to plead for her life. I was going to request that you use my weapon. I think we can all agree that it's time for us to eliminate this venomous snake from our midst. There's no use in allowing her to live so she can continue her attacks on us.

Marisol got her designer handbag and retrieved her weapon. The rest of the women stood to their feet and began moving toward the other three women who had surrounded Rosalinda. Marisol handed the weapon to Ana.

Rosalinda's body trembled as they began their approach. Terror flashed in her eyes. The hairs on the back of her neck were rising. She turned to face the women. Hoping to gain sympathy from the group, she tried pleading for her life, but she had difficulty speaking as her mouth was as dry as a desert floor. With a hoarsened voice and stammering on broken words, she said,

"I…I'm so sorry. I really am. Pl…Please don't do this. Just let me go. You'll never have any trouble out of me again."

"There's no excuse for what you've done to me. I heard everything you said and the bitter, vitriolic tone when saying it. I mean, you were downright indignant, as if I'd offended you or caused you harm. If you feel this way, there's no telling what you'll do to me. Now I see the hatred in your heart towards me. I can't trust you. I don't need anyone in my circle who's willing to stab me in the back. Next, you'll try to have me murdered. You try to get my friends here to turn on me. Then I hear you speak evil of my boys when I've protected yours. No doubt you've trained them to hate me as well. Not only are you going to die today, but I'll also have your little raped-produced bastards rounded up, and they will be exterminated right along with their mama, the snake."

With the threat of her sons dying at the hands of Ana, Rosalinda tried to stand to plead for their lives, but her legs weakened and gave way, causing her to fall in her chair. Her hands shook violently as she took a quick puff from her cigar. She was still holding the playing cards in her other hand.

Her heart raced rapidly as she faced her soon-to-be killer. She tried once more to plead for her life in hopes that she would be spared, but seeing the hardened, evil stare of her former friend, she knew her fate was sealed. She could only brace herself for the inevitable.

The women in the room began to inch slowly towards her, so slow that she welcomed a quick death, for the fear and dread she felt seemed far worse than dying. She watched as Ana took Marisol's weapon, her right hand firmly clasped around the handle of the Glock seventeen, and she aimed it towards Rosalinda. The loud pop broke the silence in the room. The woman yelled in pain as the bullet landed in her upper body. The blast knocked her to the floor, where her body landed at Ana's feet. Rosalinda's hand trembled as she reached for the open wound while gasping for air.

Distorted voices of evil swirled through her head as her life slipped away. The weapon was handed to Marisol, who proudly fired a shot into the dying woman's upper torso. She passed it on to Isabella, who did the same. They continued to pass the weapon until each lady had partaken in the killing. After the murder, Isabella, trying not to step in Rosalinda's blood so as not to damage her fifteen-hundred-dollar designer shoes, bent over and picked up the deceased woman's cigar. She took a puff from it. She then picked up the playing cards that had fallen to the floor. "Humph; a bad hand, I see. Guess she wasn't so lucky."

The ladies returned to their seats as Rosalinda's body lay on the floor, reduced to a hundred and sixty pounds of bloody mass. The room was filled with laughter as the ladies ate their meals, got tipsy, and finished their card games. Relieved that Rosalinda was dead, they were able to enjoy their event without the drama she brought to the group. Marisol lifted her glass and shouted, "Los Zorro's Blanco!"

"Los Zorro's Blanco!" the ladies shouted in unison. After enjoying their evening, they were escorted to their limos. The head of Ana's security team, Alberto, motioned for a couple of underlings to get the cleaning supplies so they could dispose of Rosalinda's body. "Hey boys, come and help get the old bitch cleaned up. Take her to the usual spot." Rosalinda was taken to an incinerator along with her sons, who had also been murdered. The incident was never spoken of again.

CHAPTER ONE

It was the day after Christmas; remnants of snow lay on the surface of the lawns of a picturesque, serene, upscale neighborhood in west Little Rock. Ice sickles hung from the rooftops of posh modern Mediterranean-styled homes on the bitterly cold morning. The crackling of wood could be heard burning softly in the large fireplace, a soothing melody that brought comfort to its guests. The scent of freshly brewed coffee and faint smells of a gourmet breakfast blended into harmonious notes of aromatic bliss. The lights flickered on the tree with ornaments perfectly hung in place. It was empty underneath; all gifts had been given to their intended recipients. Leftovers from Christmas dinner had finally been put away, and the housekeeper had taken out the last of the gift wrappings and other trash.

The hustle and bustle of the busy holiday season was finally over, and Cindy couldn't be happier. She warmed herself by the fireplace. She wore her favorite silk pajamas and cozy slippers. Her hair was neatly braided into one long French braid. She wore no make-up, signaling she was prepared to do absolutely nothing but relax with her man.

Sipping a cup of hot chocolate, she looked across the room where, on the sofa, lay her expectant cousin Amber, who was relaxing and caressing her tiny belly bump. She was full from the breakfast they all had just consumed. Her blonde hair was tousled about and looked unkempt; she too was exhausted and winding down from the busyness of the holiday season. Cindy's boyfriend, Blaine, joined Cindy and Amber in the massive den. He was planted on the sofa, finishing a cup of coffee. He was watching Cindy as she stood by the fireplace, warming herself. He motioned for her to come and sit next to him on the large sofa so they could enjoy the warmth of the fireplace together.

"Damn baby," he said, admiring her look of simplicity. She wore no glamourous make-up, no extravagant hairstyles or larger-than-life costumes, only her natural beauty. He could see the outline of her toned ass through the pajamas. Her nipples protruded through the soft fabric. He began salivating, wanting to place them in his mouth. He expressed his mannish charm, not caring who was listening.

"You're the only woman I know who can make PJs look sexy. Girl, you've got my damn mouth watering. Little Jimmy's down here hard as steel," he said, rubbing his stiff muscle. His naughty smile revealed the dimples on his handsome face. "Bring your sexy ass over here."

"Alright now; you'd better behave. You're going to get into trouble talking like that," she said with a flirtatious smile. She loved it when he flirted with her.

"Oh, I like a little trouble now and then," he said. "Especially if you're dishing out the punishment. But seriously babe, I love seeing you like this, at home doing nothing but resting. You seem to be at peace. You're always so busy with the club. You rarely take any time off. I thought you two ladies would be off with the rest of the women in Little Rock shopping and returning gifts." Cindy, produced a slight frown while making her way to the sofa, said,

"Baby, it's not that serious. I've been working hard all week long, and I've shopped for my family, employees, and friends, and there's no way in hell I'm prepared to go through that circus act. Shit, they can have it. It's not worth it. If I didn't get it before Christmas, it's not going to make one damn bit of difference today. Besides, it's cold as heck out there."

"But I don't get it. I thought all women loved to shop," Blaine replied, looking baffled.

"I love shopping, but I hate crowds. That's why I got my shopping done long before the holiday season. I'm not like the rest of the people out there walking around like zombies in the freezing cold over a few dollars' worth of useless crap. They could be doing what we're doing. Relaxing, keeping warm, and truly enjoying their families, but they're so Americanized that they would rather be out there with the masses than enjoying what really matters in life. For that very reason, I got all my shopping done early. I don't even want to think about that foolishness." Cindy kissed Blaine on the forehead and then gave him a quick peck on the lips before sitting next to him.

After a hefty yawn, Amber said, "They should've shopped online like I did. I had everybody's gifts sent to them by mail. I didn't even have to gift-wrap them. It saves time and energy. I simply let the online retailers do the work for me."

"Damn Amber, I should've thought of that. Perhaps I'll do that next year. Better yet, I think I'll hire someone else to do it for me."

"There you go baby; it doesn't get much easier than that. That way, you can spend the time you save lying next to me," Blaine said. Cindy finished her hot chocolate, snuggled up to Blaine, and rested her head on his shoulder.

"I'd much rather be sitting with you than out there. Besides, life's too short. I almost lost you once, and that wasn't a good thing. I want to spend as much time with you as possible," said Cindy.

"We've both had a brush with death, but the good Lord had a different plan in mind." Blaine pulled her in close, planting a few grateful kisses on her face.

After a few minutes had passed, Cindy glanced over at Amber and asked,

"Amber, what time do you plan on leaving?" She got no answer.

"Amber-r-r," she called out to her in a hushed voice, allowing her name to linger on her tongue. Amber had already fallen asleep. Cindy shifted her focus to Blaine. They shared a passionate kiss. Afterwards, they went into the bedroom for a little more privacy.

When Amber woke from her nap, she went into the guest bedroom and finished packing the rest of her things. She was leaving Arkansas to start a new life with her parents. They were moving to the California coast in Santa Catalina. She sold both her condos and purchased a four-bedroom home with a portion of the money. She inherited three million dollars from her boyfriend, a violent drug lord. Unbeknownst to her, he was killed by none other than her cousin Cindy. Amber's life was in danger, as was her own.

Cindy's ex-fiancé Anton Delgado, and Amber's deceased boyfriend, Andre, were brothers. Anton sought to rekindle his and Cindy's past relationship, but when she declined, he began bullying her and killing anyone who got in his way. Anton's hired hitman named Wolf killed Cindy's son. A few of her friends and employees were killed in an attempt to take over her business. Tired of living with the constant threats, she killed him. She knew the police could do nothing to help her, and even if he was arrested, he could've easily run his criminal organization from behind bars. Her only recourse *was* to kill him. Not only did she kill him and his brother, but many of his hired goons.

Although Amber didn't know Cindy was responsible for the death of her boyfriend, she *was* present when Anton was killed.

Cindy wasn't charged, and the deaths were deemed justified. The Delgado brothers were survived by their only living relative their mother. Cindy knew as long as their mother was alive, there was a possibility that Amber and her baby were not going to be safe. As a precaution, Amber and her parents were leaving town. She had three million dollars to start over and planned on lying low until Mrs. Delgado died. Amber was to get more money from the Delgado estate once the baby was born, but Cindy convinced her to leave the baby's share of the money and skip town. As Amber was finishing her packing, Cindy walked into the room.

"Need some help?"

"No, I think I just about got everything," Amber said, trying to zip the stuffed suitcase. Cindy walked over and pressed the suitcase while Amber finally got it zipped.

Afterwards, Amber sat on the bed, her eyes dropping to the floor and staring into nothingness. She didn't like the fact that she had to hide out, especially since she'd dropped out of law school to fulfill her dreams of becoming an actor. She now had to put her life on hold for her safety and that of her unborn child. Cindy knew she didn't want to leave, so she tried her best to cheer her up. Sitting next to her, she took her hand.

"Hey doll, it's only temporary."

"I know, but it seems so drastic to just up and leave everything, especially for Mom and Dad."

"It's for the best. Ana Maria Delgado is just as dangerous as her sons were. I should know. I was a part of that family for years. I'm afraid your life may still be in danger, especially if she knows about the baby. I hate to sound like a broken record, but I advised you not to tell that family about the pregnancy. You told Anton and his attorney because you wanted the money. I can understand you want a better financial future for your child, but this was not the way to go about it. I knew revealing this baby to them would keep them in our lives forever. I know how they operate. The family is very selfish, and they don't know the meaning of the

18

word, no. They're very controlling, manipulating killers. You witnessed what happened back at the house in Mayflower. Anton had planned to kill us both. He had already sexually assaulted you. How do you rape the pregnant girlfriend of your brother? That family has the blackest of hearts. You can never be too safe. Trust me; you're doing the right thing. Besides, your parents will be with you, and I'm always just a phone call away."

"I guess you're right," Amber said.

"Think of it as a wonderful adventure. You'll meet new people and make new friends. Look on the bright side: a home on Catalina Island. Shit, if it were not for my business, I think I'd pack up and move there myself. You're lucky you and your parents are still alive. Be grateful and move on. Count your blessings, all three million dollars of it; you have your parents, and soon you'll be holding a beautiful child. You're going to be just fine. Now give your cousin a hug." Amber leaned in, resting her head on Cindy as she gave her a half hug.

"Cindy, I want to thank you for everything you've done for me and my parents. Thank you for saving my life. I know I got myself into this trouble. My actions almost got us both killed. You put your life on the line to save mine. You repeatedly warned me, but I just had to do things my way. I'm going to listen to you from now on. Watching you kill Anton to protect us gave me a newfound respect for you. I was so afraid that day. I didn't think we were going to make it out alive. We practically had to shoot our way out of there. It was one of the worst experiences of my life, all because I had to do things my way."

"You're not totally to blame. Anton set those events in motion. He felt it was beneficial to use you to get to me. His plan got him killed. He didn't expect me to fight back. He was used to bullying others. Most people bow down to him, but he underestimated me. He thought that I was going to sit idly by and

19

let him kill my friends and family. I couldn't let that happen. I was minding my business, and he came harassing me. He's had thousands of people murdered, yet he felt he was untouchable."

"Cindy, may I ask you a question?"

"Sure; what is it?"

"Anton seemed to think that you had something to do with Andre's death. That night, when I was at the cabin, you told me to put the tracking device in Andre's phone. Not long after that, he was killed. Are you the one who killed him, or did you have him killed?"

Stoned face, Cindy looked Amber directly in the eyes and said, "Amber, I had nothing to do with the death of Andre. I don't know who killed him, but for your sake, I'm glad someone did."

She hated lying, but she knew she couldn't openly admit murdering Andre, especially not to Amber, who was known to be unstable. She couldn't risk telling anyone that she was a killer. Not only did she kill Amber's boyfriend, but she also plotted his death and many others in the Delgado organization, including Anton.

"Amber wasn't sure she wanted to believe her. She tried studying her to see if she could detect the slightest bit of deception. Looking incredulously, she exhaled and said,

"It's okay if you did." She placed her hand over Cindy's. "I'm grateful to whomever, especially if they did it to protect me."

Knowing that Amber didn't quite believe her, Cindy said, "Well, it's too bad we'll never know who it was. Now, we won't get to thank them."

"Cindy, I love you so much."

"I love you too. Now take good care of my aunt and uncle and your baby. Remember to never call me at home or at the club.

Only use our burner phones when you want to talk." While they were talking, Amber's car pulled up and tooted the horn.

"Well, I guess it's about that time," Amber said. She gripped her cousin as if it were the very last time she would see her. She studied her face to remember her. She slowly walked out of the spare bedroom and went to the carport. Blaine helped with her bags. When she was seated in the vehicle, Cindy leaned in and said, "Take care of yourself, cousin. I'll see you soon."

"I love you Cindy," Amber said through tears."

"I know sweetie."

Cindy kissed her, closed the door, and went inside. She was a bit emotional about her family's departure, but she knew it was for the best. She went into her home and rested in the arms of her lover.

Four Months later.......

Sitting in his large posh office with a preppy look, Santiago Burkett ran his fingers through his thick dark hair, which was professionally cut and styled to perfection. His chiseled good looks and strong facial features gave him the appearance of a male fashion model, a product of a Cuban mother and a Caucasian father. His navy-blue Brunello Cuccinelli suit made him look every bit the distinguished, prominent attorney. With deep blue eyes, he looked down his slender nose and leaned over the conference table to address his client, an elderly Cuban lady. Her name; Ana Maria Delgado. She was beautiful with her deep bronze complexion and friendly, grandmotherly appearance. Although she looked innocent, she was far from it. She was quite the opposite; she was deadly.

Still grieving the deaths of her sons, she was conservative in her appearance. She wore no fancy clothing to showcase her wealth, no expensive jewelry, just a simple pair of diamond studs and minimal make-up. Her silver hair was neatly pinned in a bun, and her apparel, although expensive, was plain. She'd been crying all morning, dreading the visit.

She had come to Arkansas to finalize the accounts of both her sons' financial affairs. This would be the last thing she would do for her children. With her purse resting on her lap, her slightly wrinkled left hand that clutched the straps still bore the wedding ring that her late husband had given her. She wore a diamond-encrusted, heart-shaped vial around her neck that she touched every few minutes. The vial contained the ashes of her sons, her husband, and her father-in-law mingled together. Three generations of Delgado men had been reduced to ashes. She gripped it tightly with her right hand. Her mind wandered, thinking of her sons, until her attorney broke her train of thought.

"Mrs. Delgado, assets owned by Anton have been merged into the Delgado accounts. The clubs that were destroyed in Miami and the land that the big house sat on can either be put up for sale, or you can rebuild. You have several options. Let me know your decision, and I'll make it happen. The remaining clubs are thriving as well as the Delgado Company." With compassion in his voice, the lawyer said,

"Mrs. Delgado, you've suffered a great loss. I'm saddened by all that's happened. I want to assure you that we're acting in the company's best interest. Naming a new CEO can wait until you're ready. No one can ever replace your sons. When the time is right, we'll find a suitable candidate. Preferably someone within the company who already knows the business, someone who has as much drive and passion as the brothers. As you know, Anton had no children. I searched everywhere but came up empty." The woman was emotional.

Ana Maria was known in her circle to be tough as nails, and she ruled her criminal organization with an iron fist, but when it came to the death of her sons, she was as weak as any other mother who had lost a child. Disappointment showed on her face as she heard the finality of his statement. *"Anton had no children."* She let those words sink in for a few seconds. Her heart ached. Santiago handed her a tissue, which she used to blot the tears that streamed down her face.

Ana Maria Delgado is the wife of Hector, the only son of Ernesto Delgado. They were one of the most notorious crime families to ever come out of Cuba. She was a major player in the Delgado organization and ran the business with her father-in-law. Their crime syndicate began its reign in Cuba and eventually expanded worldwide. Their order of business was dealing in arms and narcotics sales in Miami. Their criminal activities weren't limited to weapons and narcotic sales but included anything that could bring them a profit. If it were illegal, they were into it. They conducted business with other criminals of like mind regardless of race or nationality. The source of the money wasn't an issue; all money was good money as far as the Delgados were concerned.

At the age of seventeen, Ana Maria met her father-in-law, Ernesto, in a local tavern where she was a waitress. He noticed she was very beautiful. He watched her from afar as she worked the place, scouting potential clients vacationing in Cuba who were possibly looking for sex.

She slept with many of her customers to secure extra cash to provide for her and her best friend. In a drunken stupor, a bar patron began groping her. An argument ensued, and the customer violently slapped her. She took a straight razor from her bra and slit his throat. He fell to the floor, holding his neck. As blood gushed from the gaping wound, she continued serving her customers as if she hadn't done a thing.

She wasn't charged in the incident because Ernesto, armed with influence and extreme power, intervened on her behalf. He admired how she handled herself in the incident and was curious as to how cold the teen was afterwards, not caring if her target lived or died. The incident was done swiftly, so swiftly, the guy she'd cut hadn't realized it until he began gasping for air. Ernesto befriended her and took her with him that evening.

After learning more about her, he began to recruit her for his criminal organization. He enjoyed her youthful beauty and began spoiling her, showering her with the best gifts a man of his means could provide. She warmed up to the older man and began to fall in love with him. They shared a brief romance, but he knew they couldn't continue the relationship, not for what he had in mind. Falling in love with her would destroy his plan, and he'd kill someone for sure if his heartstrings were attached. Instead, he trained her in the art of killing. Hiding beneath the exterior of innocence and youth was a hardcore street-smart killer. She exhibited the characteristics of a humble, meek servant catering to her clients' egos. Men felt safe around her, even letting down their guards as they began to trust her. She had a body that rendered any man helpless, an effective seductress who was skilled in the art of sex. She was invited to major events with powerful men as an escort. She quietly sat in the background, eavesdropping on her clients while gaining access to their business plans. She would then send the information back to her boss. In the beginning, Ernesto assigned Ana Maria to minor jobs. After proving her loyalty, she was given better, higher-profile assignments.

Ernesto had many beautiful women working for him, but Ana Maria was his powerful, most effective weapon. He gave her the moniker; "Hermosa Asesina" or "Beautiful Assassin." Among the many gifts he'd given her, the one she cherished the most was a .32 Saturday night special, which she used to kill her prey. It was chrome with a white pearl handle. He also provided her with a designer switchblade. She loved it because it was quick and quiet and brought no unwanted attention. Now a professional with many successes under her hat, she was used for almost everything from helping to close major financial deals to debt collections and even murder, which was now her specialty. She was able to get close to unsuspecting targets, assassinate them, and collect her fare.

She was responsible for the deaths of many rivals of the Delgado organization, especially in the early days. Because of her success, she began moving up in the ranks of the syndicate. She showed great passion for the business.

Ana Maria's parents were viciously murdered in Cuba during the Batista and Castro eras. Working for Ernesto gave her a sense of belonging and protection, and it was far better than working on her own. He trusted her with his empire, and with her assistance, he reigned in the region. She became second in command only to him.

He found her more honorable than his son, who lacked passion or vision for the family business. He was spoiled and used to having everything handed to him by his father.

Ana Maria knew what it was like to have nothing, and she appreciated the opportunities given to her by Ernesto. After years of closely monitoring her, he felt that in the event of his death, he could trust her to carry on in his stead, and the business would be okay under her order. To ensure the money remained with the Delgado family, he suggested that she marry his son, which she did out of loyalty to Ernesto. Two sons were born from the union.

Her best friend Isabella, whose parents were also killed in the same ambush that killed her parents, worked with the organization alongside Ana Maria, who carefully recruited her. Isabella moved with the Delgados to America, settling in Miami. She met her husband Walter Burkett, a prestigious but very crooked attorney, who was in Miami on business for the Delgado family. They fell in love and were married a year later. Their son, Santiago Burkett, was born.

Ernesto died of a heart attack after the move to America. Hector, his son, was known for cheating on Ana Maria, often having wild, drunken cocaine parties with beautiful women. He began to get sloppy with a few drug deals, and soon, the feds were on his trail. When threatened with prison, he struck a deal and testified against his rivals and old acquaintances. He even testified against a few of his father's allies. He ratted out everyone, small or great. The feds had no case without his testimony. He gave names, dates, bodies, and shipment information. He gave up Anything they needed, and in turn, he received a year in jail, a mere slap on the wrist, and he and his family entered into the federal witness protection program. When he thought the dust had settled, he made a trip to Cuba, where he was quickly found and assassinated.

After his death, Ana Maria and her sons carried the family business even further, obtaining several legitimate businesses, netting them millions of dollars. Because the Colombian drug trade and illegal arms deals were such a lucrative source of income, they found it difficult to steer clear of the criminal side of the business.

They were vicious killers, including Ana Maria, who was the most violent of them all. Although she was the ringleader, she quietly stood in the background while her sons and others carried out her orders in the Delgado cartel.

Now she sits in her attorney's office, Santiago Burkett, the son of her best friend Isabella. Nursing her broken heart, she shrugged her shoulders and asked,

"What am I to do? I have no more sons to carry on the Delgado name. My last living son's legacy was snuffed out by that lying puta Cindy Brooks. She killed my boy and has never done a day in prison, but I'm going to make her pay. The police stood by while she took his life, and now, I'm alone. My dear Hector is gone, and so is my baby boy Andre, and now there's nobody left."

"Actually, Mrs. Delgado, that's not entirely true. Did Anton mention to you that Andre has a child on the way?"

Stunned by the news, she stopped sobbing and focused her eyes on Santiago with an inquisitive expression. She could tell by the tone of his voice and the structure of his words that what he was about to tell her would give her hope. Sitting on the edge of her seat, she waited for him to explain in detail.

"Mrs. Delgado, before Anton was killed, we were in the process of finalizing Andre's living will. We hadn't gotten a chance to finish because he died a month later. There's a young lady whom Andre was quite fond of. Her name is Amber Brooks. She was his girlfriend. He left her a genuinely nice sum of money, three million dollars to be exact. Anton honored his brother's last request and let her have the money. There was a stipulation in the will that if she had his child, she would get even more. She came to the reading of the will of which Anton and my secretary were in attendance. You were still grieving at the time, so Anton handled his brother's final financial affairs."

"So, what are you saying?" she asked anxiously.

"This young lady is pregnant with Andre's child. I believe she's in her last trimester. She's received her share of the inheritance, but she can't claim the baby's share until after the birth. Over the last few months, I've been trying to contact her to assist her with the baby's trust, but to no avail. The phone number I have for her has been disconnected, and I can't seem to find a forwarding address on her anywhere."

The lady stood to her feet. She quickly went from a grieving mother to falling back into her role as the murderous leader of the cartel. She was ready to make someone pay for keeping her in the dark.

"So, it never occurred to my son or anyone else to inform me of this news? Must I find out this? Now, here you sit telling me that there's a possibility of me having a grandchild, and you can't find the mother? That's unacceptable, Santiago. I built this organization. No one spoke with me about large sums of money leaving my business. Why was this transaction cleared, and I was not informed? No amount of money should've left those accounts without my approval.

"With all due respect, Mrs. Delgado, I assumed you already knew, and as far as the money being taken from the accounts, Anton handled that particular transaction himself. I was simply here to document it. As I said, out of respect, we knew you were in mourning, so Anton did what he thought was best. I tried tracing the money, hoping she would leave a trail, but I didn't get far. The account she used was closed after she withdrew all the funds."

"This girl screwed my son, takes my money, and doesn't even try to contact me about my grandchild. How selfish can she be? Find her, my money, and my grandchild. If you can't, then perhaps your father can. Does Isabella know about this?"

"No, I haven't mentioned it to her."

"What about Burkett does he know?"

"I haven't mentioned it to him either. No matter how close we are, I don't discuss my client's business with my parents. Besides, Father was busy with his clients and preparing for the big Ramone trial. I don't need to tell you how important that is."

"I understand the trial is important because it affects a large portion of my business, but this situation is just as important. I want that girl. I want to know everything about her."

Santiago was worried for Amber. He knew she was in danger and immediately regretted mentioning the subject, especially since Ana Maria knew nothing about the baby. She wasn't the only person to worry about concerning Amber. His own father, a corrupt former politician having served two terms as a state representative and a close friend of the Delgado family, is deeply involved in their criminal organization. Now a prominent defense attorney, he assists anyone in the Delgado crime syndicate to escape convictions getting them off on any charges of witness tampering, murder, and destroying evidence. The Delgados used his services often, and having been in the political arena, the Delgado & Burkett organization was known for lining the pockets of many corrupt public officials.

Ana Maria stood to her feet and said, "Find this girl because I want that child as soon as it's born. Pay whatever you must to get her to go away, but I want my grandchild."

"Mrs. Delgado, I'm sure she loves this child already. She won't simply give her child up."

"She doesn't have a choice in the matter. Either she gives me the child as soon as it's born, or I'll kill her. Either way, the child is mine. I had planned on going back to Miami, but I'm going to stay here until we find my grandchild. I want to take him or her back to Miami with me."

She walked towards the door, where her armed bodyguard, Luis, stood waiting. Luis, a large, robust Cuban male in his late forties, had been with her for twenty years. He opened the door for her. She stormed out of the office, and Luis followed behind her. She quickly called Santiago's father, Walter.

Santiago could faintly hear her phone call, and he was worried for Amber. Not only was he worried for Amber, but also for her cousin Cindy. There would be more bloodshed, and he was growing tired of it. He knew Cindy personally from when she and Anton were together. He attended the engagement party that Ana Maria hosted for them. He'd recently met Amber after the death of Andre at the reading and distribution of the funds of the will.

Santiago grew up in Arkansas after his mother, Isabella, followed Ana Maria and her husband, who had been relocated there in the witness protection program. The two women were like sisters. He and the Delgado boys were around the same age, and because they were closely knit, they spent family times together and enjoyed hanging out. Santiago's parents knew early on that the Delgados would be grooming their boys for the family business, and they were destined to live a life of crime.

Due to the nature of his parents' involvement with the Delgado crime family, they sent him away to an elite boarding school for boys in New York. During his teens, he was sent to London until his undergrad. They didn't want him involved in the business. They wanted him to get the best education, and it would be worth the investment, especially since he was intelligent. He was obsessed with school. He tried to bury himself in his studies in hopes he could forget the things he knew about his parents and their friends.

Finally, he moved to Cambridge, Massachusetts, where his father, Walter, hired a wealthy host family to look after him. His father was adamant that he gets a law degree, which he obtained from Harvard.

Santiago was the better part of his family. Since he didn't grow up in the criminal underworld, he tried to avoid his father's friends who were. He felt forced by his father to work with him at his law firm in Sherwood, Arkansas. He knew the consequences would be great if he didn't comply, so he did as he was told. He would've much preferred to work in a large city more suited to his talent. He felt limited in Arkansas. His father only used his services to further his criminal empire and help his friends.

He'd witnessed his parents in action and knew they were just as dangerous as Ana Maria. He didn't want anything to happen to Amber, her unborn child, or Cindy. He saw Cindy and Amber as two unfortunate girls who'd gotten caught up in the wrong family. He immediately sought Cindy out. He knew she wouldn't tell him the whereabouts of Amber because he had already tried. He now wanted to get a warning to her that Ana Maria was back, and she was furious.

Cindy's Soiree Club

It was Thursday evening, and Cindy and her employees were getting ready for the nightly shows. Cindy's Soiree Club was a restaurant and a cabaret located in Little Rock. She put on grand burlesque-styled erotic shows with Spoken Word, comedy, and other performances. There was plenty of entertainment for her adult patrons. The place was popular, and many celebrities and entertainers have either performed there or dined there. Patrons flew in from all over to enjoy the finest five-star meals created by Cindy's very own celebrity chef and an array of imported wines and sexy entertainment. The entertainers were getting into their costumes and make-up. Cindy was walking through, ensuring everything was on point and everyone was on their post. She was sampling foods and putting the finishing touches on her makeup. She heard her name being called.

"Cindy, there's a very handsome young man out front who's asking for you." She looked at the young bartender and asked,

"Well, did you get his name?"

"He didn't give a name. He just said it was urgent."

"You know how busy we are; tell him to come back later."

"I tried that already. He said it was urgent, and he wouldn't take no for an answer."

A little frustrated, Cindy went to the dining area of the club. When she saw it was Santiago, she thought it was another attempt to have her reveal Amber's whereabouts. She didn't have the time or the desire for the discussion, but tonight, he'd come to give her a warning.

He watched as she walked towards him. She was wearing a sexy but elegant cream and lace dress. The bust and waist were covered in sequins. Her long dark hair that reached her curvy buttocks was loosely curled and swooped to one side. Her make-up was flawless. She wore a very sexy pair of high-heeled sandals and exquisite costume jewelry. He was stunned when she walked out looking so beautiful. His mouth hung open in awe of her. He began to think just how lucky Anton Delgado had been just to have had her as his lover. She was always beautiful to him and seemed to look even better the more she matured. Cindy looked at him and asked,

"So, are you just going to stand there with your mouth open or are you going to tell me the nature of your visit? And I need you to hurry because I have a business to run. If you're looking for Amber, don't waste your time, she wants nothing of the money. She's doing quite well."

Once he regained his composure from lustfully staring at her, he had a look of worry on his face. Cindy could tell something was bothering him.

"Let's have a seat over here where we can talk privately." They were seated.

"I hate to bother you Cindy, but I need to get an urgent message to Amber."

"What's going on Santiago?"

"Mrs. Delgado came by my office today to tie up the loose ends on her sons' estates. I just so happened to mention Amber's pregnancy. I had no idea she didn't know about the baby. I was under the impression that Anton had already mentioned it to her. She admitted that she knew nothing about the baby and immediately became obsessed with me finding her. She wants Amber to have the baby and turn it over to her. She says if she doesn't hand over her child immediately, she will kill her and take the baby anyway."

Cindy was disheartened at the news, but she'd prepared Amber for this very reason.

"I knew this baby was bad news the moment Amber told me she was pregnant. I told her not to tell anyone, but she had to be hard-headed. I knew this would happen if that family found out about the baby. First, it was Anton, now it's his mother. I mean, why won't that family just die already? I'm so sick of them. They're so evil. They've managed to do irreparable harm to me for many years. It's like they will never go away. They're always causing problems, and now Amber has one growing inside of her. I can only hope he or she doesn't turn out like them."

"Cindy, Mrs. Delgado is very serious about the child. She thinks I'm not doing enough to find her, so she's getting my parents involved, and I don't need to tell you how dangerous of a combination that will be. I grew up with the Delgados but I'm nothing like them or my parents. Once they learn about the situation, they'll find her. Mrs. Delgado is gunning for you, too. She wants your blood for the blood of her son. I think you need to take the necessary precautions to protect yourself. I don't want any more bloodshed towards you or your family from these people. You'd think she would be tired by now, but as far as Mrs. Delgado is concerned, she's not going to let this thing go."

Cindy looked worried. She wasn't afraid for her life but for her family. She knew Ana Maria wasn't going to give up. She was tired of being afraid, and she wasn't going to run or hide. If Ana Maria wanted her, she would have to come and get her. She was glad that Amber had already left town.

"Santiago, thank you for letting me know. Amber's in a safe place. I'm not worried about my life. I got tired of running a long time ago. Ana Maria wants a fucking bloodbath. I'm going to have to give her one, especially when it comes to my family. I didn't let her son bully me, and I'm damn sure not about to let her do it.

Fuck her. She'll be alright, and she will not get her damn grimy hands on that baby. Everything she touches, she destroys. What type of mother grooms her own children for a life of crime? She thinks she's going to do that to Amber's child. The baby's blood is tainted with Delgado's blood, but I'll be damned if I let her taint his life with her bullshit. You tell that old bitch I said she can go and fuck herself."

Santiago shook his head. He knew giving such a message to Ana Maria would be dangerous, and he didn't want any trouble. He only wanted to warn Cindy and Amber, and he was already overstepping his bounds by doing so. If his parents or Ana Maria knew he was there, he would be killed. He replied to her comment.

"I feel the same as you, but you know she and my mother are like sisters. I'm already in this deeper than I want to be. Now my mother is going to pressure me to find her."

"Santiago, I know your mother personally. Although she can be a dangerous woman, I've always admired and respected her. She reminds me a lot of myself. I was into a lot of things when I was younger, and I, too, was what you would consider a little on the dangerous side, but I never subjected my son to my lifestyle. I did everything in my power to keep him safe. That's the way your mother did with you. I watched how she always looked out for you, and she kept you out of a lot of things. Although she's deep in the organization, her role as a mother was an honorable one. She didn't groom you to be a criminal like Ana Maria did with her sons. As much as she loves Ana Maria, her true loyalty lies with you. You can get to her. She'll listen to you. Now, your father, that's another story. Walter Burkett is as crooked as they come. He's blinded by money, and he'll kill anyone who gets in his or Mrs. Delgado's way. I can't quite understand his loyalty to her, and I don't suppose to try to figure it out. When I got out of that family, I kept going, and I never looked back until Amber showed up with Andre out of the blue. That's what brought Anton back

35

into my life. I had moved on, built my own business, and was doing great. Amber brought him to my place of business, and it all went downhill from there. I thought that with him being dead, everything would be okay, but this baby hasn't even been born yet and has already been the source of contention. I've informed Amber that she is to stay away from the Delgado organization. I've even suggested that she not give the baby the last name of its father. That name is synonymous with crime and hate. Amber needs to raise him in a good Christian atmosphere surrounded by love and honor, not drug trafficking, murder, and guns. You and I have witnessed many things in that evil family. Now Ana Maria wants to take this child and teach him about the business. That's no life for a child."

"As I said, I agree with you. I just wanted to warn you. Now I won't look for Amber, but you need to know that Mrs. Delgado is not going to give up until she's found."

"I thank you for the warning, but she's already in a safe place." Santiago stood to his feet. Cindy removed herself from the table standing face to face with him. He took her by the hand and said,

"I'm going to do everything I can to help. I'll keep you informed."

"Thank you, Santiago. I trust that you will."

She walked him to the club's entrance and watched as he got into his stylish silver Aston Martin. As he drove away, she contacted Amber to inform her about the visit and Ana Maria's plans. She got no answer, so she left a voicemail and marked it as urgent.

CHAPTER TWO

Amber had settled into her new home on the island. She had wonderful views of Avalon Bay. She often eased her mind by lounging on her patio, watching the sun rise, or strolling the beach with her parents. She was entering her ninth month of pregnancy. Although there were plenty of things to do on the island, she was limited in her activities due to her late stage of pregnancy.

It was early Saturday morning, and she was nesting. She had been preparing the nursery and getting the baby's things in order. She was planning a home birth and found the perfect doctor to assist her. Since she had only a few weeks left in her pregnancy, she wanted to get out for some fresh air and some last-minute shopping. She and her mother took the express boat to Long Beach while her father was out on a fishing boat.

Amber's parents were up in age when she was born. Now they're in their early seventies and have already retired. They'd been planning to retire to a nice, warm location, but they never thought they could afford it. After learning about what Cindy and Amber suffered at the hands of the Delgados, her parents knew they had to leave home due to the possibility of their lives being in danger. Cindy convinced them that it was for the best. They took this opportunity to try to enjoy the rest of their lives with their daughter. Cindy had a few connections of her own in law enforcement that helped them get new identities.

"Mother, when we're done shopping, how about going to Avalon and lying around in the sun so we can get tans."

"I love the sun, but I'm too old to be out there all day. I think I'd rather get on the boat with your father for a little fishing. Besides, what would I do out there while you're out there half-naked in your skimpy little bathing suit? I'll leave that up to you young girls."

She playfully fluffed her greying brunette hair as if she were Mae West from one of her movies in the 1930s and said,

"You know I'm an old-fashioned southern girl. I can't let the men see my gorgeous body; besides, your father would have a fit." Her eyes that donned crow's feet lit up as she laughed.

"But you go and enjoy yourself. The sun will be good for you."

"I don't want to go alone, Mother. You know I can't be too careful; remember why we're here."

"I don't think anyone will bother us here. Cindy and her friends have taken care of everything for us. You don't have anything to worry about."

"Well, if you won't go with me, then I'll join you and Dad."

They continued shopping and finally returned to the island. When they got home, her father had already docked the boat and brought in his load. He caught black sea bass and a few other fish. Amber went into the kitchen and saw the fish in the sink. Her father was cleaning the last of the fish. She went to hug him, but he reeked of raw fish. She could tell he was thrilled about having had a successful day.

"Dad, what do you have here?"

"Oh, just a little something I caught while out on the water today."

"They look very nice. When you're done cleaning them, Mom and I will cook them for dinner if you want."

"That would be great," he said.

Amber put her shopping bags away and showered. She put on a nice, cool sundress and a pair of flip-flops and went to the kitchen to help her mother with dinner.

"So, Mom, I was thinking we could fire up the grill and cook these while hanging out on the patio. I think it would make for a nice evening. We can put some vegetables on the grill as well, so we won't have to be in a hot kitchen. Afterwards, we can have some gelato and watch the sunset."

"That sounds great, baby. I'm sure your father would love it. You start on this salad, and I'll go and get your father's pillows. You know he'll need them for his back. These patio chairs sit a little low."

Amber's father worked for the post office his entire working career. He walked many miles over the years; sometimes, his back would give him problems. Other than that, he was in perfect health. As an African American male, he knew the risks of high blood pressure, so he ate a balanced diet and took great care of himself, especially during his early thirties. That's when his father died of heart disease and his mother from diabetes.

While her father relaxed on the patio, Amber and her mother seasoned the fish and vegetables and placed them on the grill. They engaged in a little small talk when Cindy's name was mentioned. Amber hadn't heard from Cindy in a couple of weeks, so she wanted to give her a call to see how she was doing. She went into her bedroom to get her cell phone. She noticed that Cindy had already called. She listened to her voicemail and immediately returned her call. Cindy picked up on the first ring.

"Hello Amber"

"Hi cousin"

"Amber, this isn't a formal call. I want to let you know that Santiago stopped by."

"Well, what did he want? Is it about the money for the baby?"

"No, he stopped by to warn me that Ana Maria knows about the baby. She told Santiago to find you and have you turn the baby over to her after it's born. She says if you don't, she is willing to harm you. I'm calling you to warn you to watch yourself out there. Be on guard against anyone or anything suspicious. She won't stop until she's found you. She has Santiago's father, Walter, on the case, so it's only a matter of time before they track you down. The only people who know about you and your parents' new identity are me, Blaine, Jessica Barnes, and a few people at the police department who assisted us. I don't believe any of the guys at the L.R.P.D. are corrupt, at least not the ones we worked with, but still, I feel a little uneasy. I think Santiago is on our side, but I can't be too sure. I need you to lay low and stay safe."

Alarmed at the news, Amber immediately lost her appetite. She was distraught.

"Oh, Cindy when is this going to end? I thought this would be over with soon. I can't do this. What am I supposed to do now? I'm so afraid."

She now regrets telling anyone about the baby. A sharp pain shot through her lower abdomen and the lower part of her back. Gritting her teeth from the pain, she said,

"Cindy, I have to go. I think I'm going into labor." She dropped the phone and fell to her knees. She cried out in pain and yelled for her mother. Her father, hearing the commotion, hurried to her room. Her father walked inside the room and helped her from the floor.

"Are you alright?"

"Dad, get Mom and call my doctor. I'm going into labor," Amber eased over to the bed. Her hand cupped her belly due to the labor pains.

Her father did as she requested, running as fast as his legs could take him. After they got the doctor on the phone, Amber informed her parents of what Cindy had told her.

"I just got off the phone with Cindy. She said that Ana Maria Delgado is searching for us. She says she wants my baby, and if I don't give him over, she'll have me killed."

"Oh dear," her mother said, concerned for their safety. Fear set in after hearing about the threats.

"Can't the police do anything about her threatening you?"

"Mom if the police could help me, I wouldn't be on the run right now. That's why we had to change our names temporarily. She's a dangerous woman with major influence. She's not to be toyed with. She's actively searching for me, and I'm afraid for all of us."

Her father was alarmed, but he didn't let on. He took his daughter's hand and said, "Baby, I'm not going to let anything happen to you. I'm your father, and it's my job to protect you and your mother. We're going to be alright. Please try not to let this worry you." While they were talking, the doorbell rang.

"That should be Doctor Williams. Please check for me."

Amber's father went to the door. It was the doctor, so he let her in. She immediately went to Amber's bedside. Seeing the worry on her patient's face, she tried to comfort her. She thought her nervousness was due to being a first-time mother. She didn't know Amber had more worries than just her baby. She couldn't afford the luxury of happily bringing her baby into the world.

"I'm here, Ms. Henderson," the doctor said, calling Amber by her alias.

"Don't worry. I'll help you through this. I've delivered hundreds of babies. You'll be holding your little bundle of joy in no time."

Dr. Williams, a heavy-set Caucasian in her mid-forties, was more than just a midwife. She specialized in in-home births and was highly recommended. Amber was fortunate to help her with the birth on such short notice.

She examined Amber. She'd dilated four centimeters. She placed the monitor on her and watched the baby for a while. She also hooked up her blood pressure cuff. Amber was comforted by the doctor and her parents, but in the back of her mind were thoughts of Ana Maria. The doctor told her the baby would probably be delivered in twelve to fourteen hours. Amber called Cindy to inform her of what was happening.

In the meantime, Santiago was visiting his mother. She'd already learned about the baby from Ana Maria. She was reclining enjoying her brandy and a nice cigar specially blended to her liking. She wore a white linen pantsuit with a sheer cover with pearl jewels that hung loosely against her deep, mellowed, tanned skin. She was beautiful for her age of sixty-six. She took a puff of her cigar. As she was about to discuss Amber with Santiago, his father walked in. He's five-eight with a medium to slender build. His head of silver hair was professionally maintained, and he wore a grey designer suit, the tie matching the blue eyes he passed on to his son. He placed his briefcase on the coffee table, reached behind him, took his weapon from the holster, and placed it on the table alongside his briefcase. As he was doing so, he greeted his wife with a kiss and then spoke to Santiago.

"Hey, son how's it going?"

"Good evening, Father," Santiago said, dreading the conversation he knew was coming.

"We need to talk about that little girl Ana is looking for. Have you found her yet?"

"No sir but you can rest assured that I'm aggressively searching for her. Mrs. Delgado made it perfectly clear that I'm to find her immediately. I already have a few men on it but don't worry, we'll find her soon."

"Well, I'm going to need all the information you've gathered so we can locate her. Ana needs this done immediately. I have a few friends at the Marshal's office who owes me a few favors."

Hearing the alarming news, Santiago knew it would only be a matter of days before Amber was found. Hoping to stall his father, he said,

"I have her paperwork in my office. I'll give it to you first thing Monday morning."

"No son this can't wait until then. We need to get on this now."

"Okay, Dad." Walter looked at his wife, who was sitting on the sofa.

"Isabella, what's for dinner tonight?"

"I thought we'd go out tonight; give the cook a break. I'd like Italian, what do you think?"

"Sure," he said. Walter went to get freshened up for dinner. On his way out of the room, he looked at Santiago and said, "I expect you'll have that information for me as soon as this evening."

"I'm on it now Father," Santiago said.

His father left the room. His mother sensed something was bothering him. In her thick Cuban accent, she said,

"Son, I can see something's bothering you. Would you like to tell me what's on your mind?"

"Not really. I'm just concerned about a friend."

"Care to talk about it?"

"Not at this time mother."

Lifting a bottle of brandy, she poured herself a quarter of a cup. Just before she took a sip she said,

"Ana Maria told me she has a grandchild on the way. She told me that you met the mother is that true?"

"Yes, but only twice, once at the reading of Andre's will and the other when I gave her the check that was left for her as instructed by Anton. Since then, I haven't been able to find her."

"Well, don't worry. Your father will find her in less than a week; he always does."

"Yes Mother, that's what I'm worried about. Mrs. Delgado wants her found, and she wants this young lady to turn her baby over, and if she doesn't, she's going to kill her. That's bothering me. I mean when is all the killing going to stop? I'm burned out on it. Innocent people who aren't even in the business are dying, and frankly, to tell you the truth, I'm sick of it. Now I'm forced to get involved, and I really don't want any part of this. Finding and killing innocent mothers is where I draw the line, Mom. I know you and Mrs. Delgado are like sisters, and I love her too, but damn, you can't tell me that you're okay with this?"

"You watch your language, young man. Ana Maria Delgado has been more than a friend to me. She has been a provider and a protector. When I need her the most, she's always there for me. She saved my life on several occasions, even taking a bullet for me. If it wasn't for her, I'd have been dead a long time ago. You don't know the life we lived in Cuba. Life was hard on us until we met her father-in-law. She taught me the ropes and looked after me. Because of her, I met your father. Through our union, you were born. Now if Ana wants me to help her find her grandchild, who am I to keep her from that? She lost her boys; why can't we give her this grandchild? I mean I owe her that much."

"That's the thing, Mother. She lost her boys because of the business, a business that made them cruel and evil, one that changed the very dynamic of their lives from the moment they entered its trap. Now she wants to take an innocent child who might otherwise have a chance at a positive life and raise it the way she raised them. When we were young boys, we had dreams of an amazing future. Neither of us wanted to experience a life of crime. Did you know that Anton wanted to be an astronaut? He was great at science, and he was very intelligent, and then there's Andre; he wanted to serve in the military. He wanted to become an Air Force pilot. Our childhood dreams didn't consist of killing people or running a criminal organization. That was Mrs. Delgado's plan after Mr. Delgado was killed. Now they're both dead. What will come of this child once she gets her hands on him? It seems like everything that woman touches she destroys."

By then, his mother, who was a little less than five feet, stood to her feet and slapped him hard across the face.

"Don't speak of Ana like that! Not here. Not in my house. Do you hear me, son?"

Santiago was disgusted by her response. It showed in his eyes. This was the moment she greatly feared would come due to her role in the Delgado organization. Her soul ached. She was heartbroken when she realized what she'd done. She reached upwards towards his face with both hands pleading,

"I'm so sorry, son,"

She tried placing her arms around him. He hesitated then stepped away from her embrace. She insisted. He allowed her to do so, but only for a brief moment. His heart was breaking. This was his final attempt at trying to reason with her. He loved his mother, but he was truly tired of making excuses for her crimes. On the one hand, she was his inspiration for overcoming a hellacious life in Cuba and loving him and trying to raise him properly, he despised the life of crime she and his father lived. Feeling like an outsider, there were times he doubted himself due to his parents' criminal activities. He was nothing like them. He wasn't cruel and heartless. He didn't see the need to cheat, manipulate, or kill innocent people.

He whispered to her,

"Look at what she's done to you Mother. She's got you so programmed that you would abuse your own son for simply speaking the truth about her."

He looked into her soulless eyes hoping there was some way he could reach her. As always, he only saw Ana Maria Delgado deeply embedded within, as she'd sold her soul to the evil matriarch long ago. He looked past her, thinking of his childhood friends Andre and Anton, and how they were unable to live their dreams. They were doomed from birth. Angered by the heated wrath of his mother, he retorted,

"Don't worry; I'll find the girl, and I'll deliver her to you so that you can present her and her child to Mrs. Delgado; that way, their blood will be on your hands too. This is going to be my last gift to the both of you. But know this: once I deliver the girl, I'm leaving, and I don't care who you or Father hire to find me, I'll never come back here again. I've never once disrespected you or Father, and I've always done what was expected of me. I kept my mouth closed after watching you commit countless crimes against humanity, but here today you assault me because of my opinion. I understand you grew up rough and I guess you did what you felt you had to do back then. I won't pretend to understand the hell you've experienced and to your credit, you've protected me to some degree. You really should've considered what your life of crime has done to me. Living in a crime family affects those around you. I've witnessed things no child should ever have to: violent murders and torture. The falsifying of documents or setting traps for innocent people, you name it, I've witnessed it. I mean, I can't get half of those images out of my head. I'm tired. I'm walking away. I can't do this any longer, Mother. I need to be free, free of this family, this criminal organization, and this state. Perhaps I can salvage what's left of my life while I still have my sanity."

Hearing his statements, his mother was very sorrowful. Santiago poured out the rest of his thoughts in a matter of minutes. She wished she could take back what she'd done.

With tears in her eyes, she tried to apologize but she could tell by the look in his eyes she had finally lost him for good. Avoiding eye contact, he leaned in to kiss her.

"Goodbye, Mother."

"Santiago son, please; don't leave!" She pleaded.

He didn't feel the need to say anything further. He left her standing in tears and, to some degree, her own shame. He was emotionally drained and physically exhausted. As much as he loved his parents, he needed out. He knew he wouldn't make it in the organization, and sooner or later, someone was going to kill his father because he had made so many enemies. After he left, his father walked into the room refreshed and ready to go. He was humming a tune as he was buttoning the sleeve on his shirt. He saw his wife looking upset.

"What's wrong Isabella?"

"Nothing," she said trying not to cry.

"Have you been crying?"

"You know how my allergies get sometimes."

Satisfied with her answer, he grabbed his suit jacket, and she got her purse, and they left.

CHAPTER THREE

"Push! Okay, now exhale slowly," the doctor said while waiting to see the baby's head. Amber's mother was on one side and her father on the other. She gripped both of their hands. Her mother wiped the sweat from her forehead while speaking to her in a calm, soothing voice.

"You can do it, baby; It's almost over."

"Mom, I can't do it!" Amber screamed.

"Oh yes you can. You want to see that beautiful baby. Come on baby. It's almost time to push again." Dr. Williams was still in place.

"One, two, three, okay, push!" Amber pushed with all her might. She didn't feel like she was getting anywhere. She felt the harder she pushed, the less she accomplished.

"Mom, I can't. I need to go to a hospital."

"Okay, we'll take you to the hospital, but push one more time for us, okay?" Amber rested for a few more minutes. She felt an urge to push. She thought she needed to use the restroom. She informed the doctor, who convinced her to just push there on the bed.

"One, two, three, push! Oh my, I see a head." Amber's mother took a peek. Seeing her grandchild's head and face, she was overjoyed.

"One more time, Ms. Henderson."

Amber mustered up her last bit of strength and gave it all she had, and then, after a few seconds, she heard her mother say,

"It's a boy, Amber! Congratulations. He's so handsome. He has a head full of hair."

The doctor cleaned the baby's airway and lightly wrapped him while laying him on his mother. When Amber saw him, she wanted to cry. His little, wet, wriggly body squirmed. He let out a few cries and wrestled his hand free, reaching into the air as if he were seeking his mother. She comforted him.

"Oh my goodness; look at him. He is so precious." They were overjoyed. Amber, looking at her son in adoration, said,

"I'm going to do everything in my power to protect you, my sweet child."

Studying his face, her heart melted within. The cord was cut, and the doctor took the baby to weigh him and clean him further. The small separation made Amber anxious. She watched every move the doctor made. Her parents hovered over the doctor in protective mode as she continued working on him. Amber was tired and sleepy but wanted to stay awake to watch her baby.

"What will you name him?" she asked. "Will you name him after his father, perhaps?" This doctor was new to Amber, and she only knew Amber by her new name, Melinda Henderson.

"I'm going to let my father name him."

"Oh, thank you dear, but are you sure?"

"Dad, you're the most amazing man I know. You've been the best father in the world. Among men, you're the greatest. You're the epitome of what it means to be a real man. Because of you, I have come to know what it means to have a real man take care of me. As your daughter, you've spoiled me, loved me, and stood by me at my lowest point in life. You were never harsh towards me, although I may have deserved it. You're good to Mom, and demonstrating your unwavering love for her has shown me the

50

example of how a king is supposed to treat his queen. I trust you with not only my life but the life of my baby so yes, to have you name him would mean more to me than you'll ever know."

Amber's father was brought to tears by hearing her express her views of him.

"I have just the name. His first name will be that of his great-great-grandfather Patrick, meaning noble. His middle name will be Louis meaning famous warrior. My grandson will be noble, and he will fight for many. He will be loved and admired all over the earth. He will conquer anyone who tries to come against him and become a great success and the father of many sons. He will carry on the dream of his ancestors both small and great. His mother will be proud of him, and the women of this family will sing his praises."

The doctor handed him the baby. He took the child and held him close to his heart. He kissed him on the forehead, placed his hand gently on his head, and prayed,

"Father, I thank you for allowing me to live to see my grandson. I present him back to you. Use him as you see fit for your purpose and your plan. He will be great. We love you, honor you and we bless you this day."

He presented the child to his wife. She kissed him and said,

"God bless you, Patrick Louis. You will be all that God has ordained you to be, and you will accomplish His plan for your life."

She and her husband walked over to Amber's bedside. She laid the baby on Amber's chest. The baby put his hand close to his mouth and began to suck it.

"Offer him your breast, dear. He's hungry," her mother said. She breastfed him, and her life was changed. She was now a mother, and she knew her life would take on a whole new meaning. She whispered in his ear while he fed,

"I will protect you with my life. You will be safe. I won't allow anything to happen to you."

Amber and the baby slept comfortably while the doctor went about her business of taking care of mom and baby. After her work was done, she left the family alone. Amber was getting to know her baby. The doctor came and checked on him the following day. After she was satisfied that Amber and the baby were healthy, she concluded her work. She was paid in cash and went on her way. As the days went by, Amber fell more in love.

A couple of months later, on a Saturday afternoon, she was feeling a bit overwhelmed because she had been stuck in the house daily tending to her baby. She wanted to get out for a while. She gathered her and the baby's things for a trip to the beach. She protected the baby from the bright California sunshine. She finally found the perfect spot and relaxed as he slept on a soft plush mat next to her. A beautiful lady with a large hat and sunglasses walked over and took a seat next to Amber and the baby.

"He's the cutest little guy," the lady said admiring the baby.

"Thank you, ma'am,"

"He looks just like you."

"I think so too. He has hair like his father. Everything else is all me."

"What's his name?"

"His name is Patrick Louis."

"Patrick Louis," the lady said, repeating the baby's name. That sounds presidential. Perhaps he could be an important dignitary. Now, where'd you get that name?"

"My father named him."

"Well, I think it's a nice name."

The lady looked at the baby again, put her shades on her face, and lay back in her seat. Both ladies chatted for the better part of two hours while soaking up the sun. It was nearing time for the lady to leave.

"Well, I've really enjoyed your company. It was nice chatting with you," the woman said as she began packing away her things. She finally got up and left leaving one of her bags lying on the ground. Amber looked around to see if anybody was watching her. She got the bag and took it home with her. Once she got home, she went through the bag. There was a note, a set of keys, and a gift for the baby.

"Amber, here are the keys to your new apartment. Tell Aunt Nancy and Uncle Jimmy I said stay put. My friends will come and take them to their new location. The small lamb has a surprise in it. Take it with you wherever you go. After she read her instructions, she took the small stuffed animal out which had a tracking device embedded in it. Cindy was using it to track Amber and the baby. Ana Maria had finally narrowed the search down to California, so Amber and the baby were forced to leave. Her parents were relocated to a home near Nashville Tennessee. Amber was in Carson City, Nevada and she was tired of being on the run, but she was willing to do anything to ensure the safety of her baby.

She traveled in the evenings, only used cash, and stayed off the radar. Her child was almost three months old. He had an ear infection, and he needed a doctor. She was frightened. She went to an after-care clinic. Once there, she was given antibiotics. Amber was afraid to give them any information on the child because she was told to lie low, so she gave them false information. She paid the bill in cash and took a cab back to her place.

When she walked into her apartment, she immediately locked the door behind her. She placed her baby on the sofa. He was still in his car seat. She unstrapped him and held him in her arms. In the distance, she saw a shadowy figure. She thought her eyes were deceiving her but upon taking a closer look, she noticed a familiar face who was already comfortably seated. It was Santiago Burkett. He finally found her! Her heart was in her throat. A wave of nausea overtook her. She was in flight mode but was too late to run. She backed toward the entry door.

"How did you find me?"

"I simply followed Cindy. I knew she would lead me to you eventually. I mean, you guys were cautious, but the little stunt on the beach, although cute, wasn't wise. Come and have a seat. I won't hurt you; I promise." Santiago wasn't armed and he didn't appear to be dangerous, but she wasn't taking any chances. She gripped her baby, holding him close to her bosom, and asked,

"What do you want?" Are you here to take my child?"

"I was told to find you by Mrs. Delgado. Because of her close relationship with my parents, they've put a lot of pressure on me to locate you. I promised them that I would. Mrs. Delgado wants the child for herself. She's requesting that you give him over to her or she'll kill you. I'm here to tell you she's going to kill you even if you willingly give the child up. It'll be her way of tying up any loose ends as far as you're concerned. So, here's the thing: you must decide if you are going to live or die. I'm here to help you."

"So, you're not here to take my child or give me up?"

"No, I only want to help."

"What's in it for you?"

"I was born into a family of criminals. My mother and father are deep into the Delgado organization. I grew up side-by-side with Andre and Anton, and we were very close as young boys. We were like family. Their mother recruited them for the family business. She doomed them to a life of crime. My parents, however, wanted me to get a good education, so they protected me by sending me away. Over the years, Anton, Andre, and I remained friends. Anton once told me how he envied the fact that I was able to attend school and get away from the life of crime. He would beg me to steer clear of what he and his brother were doing. They truly loved me. They felt their lives had been ruined by their parents. Anton explained to me how he became a ruthless killer. He told of how his mother bullied him into killing people by slapping them around and telling them that it was how real men protected their families. She trained them to think that anyone not of the Delgado family was a potential enemy and that they should be killed if they got in the way. He was fourteen years old when Mrs. Delgado forced him to murder his first victim. He said he could never really get used to all the killing, but after a while, he said he didn't think about it anymore. By the time of his twenty-first birthday, it was second nature for him. The Delgado slogan, *"Never negotiate. Always demand your way. Kill anyone who gets in the way of family, business, or happiness,"* and that's exactly how they lived their lives. My parents live by that same motto. They may seem innocent, but they're trained killers and that's why I'm here. You're as good as dead. The only thing that I could remotely do is prolong your life for a little while. Coming from a criminal family, I know first-hand the negative effects it has on a child. My friend's lives were destroyed by their mother, and she wants to do the same to your son. I can't let that happen to another child. If my parents or Mrs. Delgado wants to live the criminal life that's on them, but to kill an innocent woman, a woman that my friend Andre cared for, I can't stand by and let that happen. I couldn't help him, but I'm going to help his child if it costs me my life. Now I told my mother that I would turn you over to them, but I can't do that. I happen to know their intentions and since I'm in charge of finding you, I'll do all I can to keep you and the baby just out of their reach, but you must cooperate with me. Do you understand?"

"How can I be sure you won't turn me over to them? How do I know you're not lying to me now?"

"It doesn't matter if I'm lying because you're dead either way so let's work with what we have today. If you run from me, you're going to be on your own. Don't try to escape because you will be found and killed. If you go to the police, you will only speed the process of your impending doom. You can do things your way or mine. Let me know because I'm prepared to walk away and leave you alone. Once they come for you, there's nothing I can do to help you. I'll bear the burden of knowing I tried to help but you refused, and then I'll be forced to watch your son grow up in a life of crime. At that time, I won't be able to do a thing about it."

Amber looked down at her baby. She thought about what he was saying, unsure if she should trust him. She had a look of desperation on her face. All he was saying actually made sense to her. He could turn her in either way. She thought long and hard.

"What should I do?"

"First you must leave here. I found you but I'm going to help you get lost again."

They got her things, and he put her in his rental car, and they left. While in the car he asked, "Do you have a way to contact Cindy anonymously?"

She pulled the burner phone out of her purse and dialed the number. Cindy answered immediately.

"Hi there, are you okay?"

"Yes, I'm scared though."

"Give me the phone!" Santiago said. She handed him the phone.

"Hey, I have them both with me and I'm going to take them to a safe location. I need to see you when I get in town. I'm going to be taking care of things as I promised you. Do you trust me?"

"Yes; actually, I do," Cindy replied.

"Okay, allow me to handle things on this end and I'll talk to you soon."

Santiago made the long, grueling trip back to Arkansas, arriving in Little Rock. Amber, who had been asleep, panicked when she saw they were crossing the city limits.

"Oh no, Santiago! You said I could trust you. You're turning me over to her. I knew you would do this to me." She became hysterical.

"Calm down, Amber. They've already searched this entire state looking for you. Everyone knows you're on the run. I know it, and so does my family, so to have you right here in the city, no one will be the wiser. The best way to hide someone is in plain sight. You'll be living in the same neighborhood that Mrs. Delgado lives in. You'll be able to keep an eye on her every day. While they're busy looking for you you'll be right under her nose." She was confused. She stared at him for a second.

"Santiago you must be crazy. Are you sure it's going to work?"

"Yes, I'm sure. She hates her neighbors, and she'll do anything she can to steer clear of most of them, so she won't even be bothered by the fact that you're there. Besides, she's always traveling to and from Miami, so you can enjoy your life with your baby right here while I run them on a wild goose chase. I'm going to leave evidence of you all over the United States. They will grow so tired of trying to hunt you down that they won't know what to do with themselves."

He laughed mischievously. Still unsure, she looked back at her baby, who was quietly resting in his car seat, then back at Santiago. She shrugged her shoulders and said,

"Oh well, I guess I have no other choice. Let's go for it."

He took her to her new home. True enough, it was only blocks away from Ana Maria's place. She could look out of her window and see the large mansion from where she was living. She had a front-row seat to the queen of the Delgado Empire.

Once she had settled in, Santiago went about his plan. He drove over to Ana Maria's home to give her a false update on Amber. Pulling his vehicle through the large wrought iron gate, he waved at security as he was allowed in. He went inside where the unmistakable smell of Cuban food permeated the air. She ushered him inside to sit and dine with her. He walked over to her and kissed her and took his place at the large Italian marble dining table. The homemade Cuban cuisine was prepared the way Santiago loved. It looked as if she had cooked it herself and he enjoyed her cooking using the perfect blend of spices and seasonings. He started with what appeared to be a simple bean and rice dish that she amped up and plantains and succulent pork dish. There was plenty of food to choose from. The aroma of the tasty dishes alone was enough to make him euphoric. He was glad he hadn't eaten, and he was ready to dive in. A place was set for him, and a glass of wine was poured for him. He took a sip of the wine and exhaled. He could tell it was about to be a great meal. He almost felt a sense of guilt because of his secret, but he saw no need not to indulge in a great home-cooked meal.

"How are you today, son?"

"I'm doing quite well," he said while unfolding his napkin and placing it on his lap.

"Does that mean you have good news for me concerning my grandchild?"

"Not quite, but I can tell you that we've narrowed our search to the west coast. It seems she opened a temporary account out there not long ago. I spoke with the bank and they're tracing her accounts and checking each time she uses her debit cards. I'll turn everything I've learned over to father. He's better at tracking than I am. I'm just a simple attorney. Father has the connections to do what I can't. I'll keep working with him until she's found. In the meantime, if you need me for anything, don't hesitate to let me know, but as for now, my father should be able to find her soon. It will only be a matter of time."

"Thank you, my dear child. You don't know how much this means to me."

"I believe I do," Santiago said. He changed the subject.

"So, Mrs. Delgado, this is a very nice neighborhood. Are the neighbors around here pretty nice?"

"I wouldn't know. I have no time for such people. They're always inviting me to things; come and join us here, we're celebrating this or that, and I hate it."

With the assurance that she doesn't know or interact with her neighbors, he felt Amber should be that much safer in the neighborhood. He continued his visit and enjoyed his meal. Afterwards, he convinced Ana Maria that he was still working on her behalf. He left.

Financial transactions were made on Amber's behalf, making it appear that she was still in the California area. He always made it appear to Ana Maria and his father that he was missing her by at least a day or two. This went on for about a year. No one suspected Santiago was helping Amber in the least.

He kept Cindy updated on Amber and the baby's progress, and from time to time, Cindy was allowed to speak with her through the constantly changing burner phones that Santiago was providing. Amber stayed in touch with her parents.

There were a couple of times that she and Cindy would pretend they were strangers. They would either sit in a park or the same restaurant, sitting in separate areas but in plain view of each other while talking on their cell phones, occasionally looking at each other. They were never allowed to really be together unless one followed the other into the ladies' restroom for a brief hug so Cindy could see the baby. It was extremely risky because they suspected that Cindy was being watched by Ana Maria, targeting her for an assassination attempt. They stopped meeting at the request of Santiago.

Santiago would constantly check on Amber and the baby who was now going on two years old and was walking and advancing. Santiago and Amber were becoming closer by the day. He was the only person she could readily see. An attraction had begun to take place between them. He went to see her one fall morning. He had pumpkin-spiced lattes, hot donuts, and apple fritters fresh from the bakery. She was sitting outside on her balcony in her sweater and enjoying the fall colors. "Hello there," he said kindly.

"I brought you a little something to warm you up on this crisp cool morning."

"What is it?" she asked out of curiosity.

"Pumpkin-spiced latte and some sweet treats for the lady."

"Ooh, you're bad. You know I'm trying to watch my figure."

She noticed he was watching her in admiration. He thought she was beautiful. The entire time he'd been protecting her; he realized that he was falling for her. Initially, out of honor and respect for Andre, he wouldn't allow his mind to go there but as time went on, he began to weaken his stance on the issue.

"From where I'm standing, I see absolutely nothing wrong with your figure. I see total perfection and beauty at its highest standards." Her face turned a bright shade of red. With flirty eyes and a shy smile, she said,

"If I didn't know any better, I would think you were flirting with me".

"Of course, I am."

He made his way over to where she was seated and handed her a cup and he took one for himself. He presented her with the box that contained the pastries. She took out what she wanted and placed it on her napkin. She took a long, slow sip of the latte. She allowed the warmth of it to rest on her tongue. The latte seemed to mingle with the morning air, and it brought a smile and pleasant thoughts. She still had yet to partake of the warm pastry that rested in her left hand. She took a bite and said,

"Santiago, you are so wrong for this. Mmm… This is so delicious!"

He watched as she enjoyed her fritter. He took a sip of his latte. He sat in the available chair. They were silent as they ate. When she finished, she said,

"This was so good. Now I'll have to run a few extra laps to undo the damage done this morning, and it's all your fault."

As she was talking, she heard Patrick Louis waking for the morning. She went to take care of him. She took his training underwear off and bathed him. Afterwards, she fed him and then put on his favorite TV show. Santiago played and sang along with him while Amber cleaned the kitchen. She smiled as she watched him making a fool of himself to please her son. After she was done with her chores, she joined them on the living room floor.

Santiago fell on his back, and Amber and the baby climbed on him, wrestling him to the floor. Patrick Louis took his little fists and balled them up, mimicking what his mother did and pretending to punch Santiago. He yelped as if he was really in pain. He finally surrendered to them both. They laughed.

Surprisingly, Amber found herself lying on his chest. Gazing into his sexy blue eyes, she thought, "Mmm….damn, *he's one gorgeous guy,*" She was grateful to him for putting his life on the line for her and her child; for sacrificing everything to protect her. Not only that, but he also spent quality time with them and didn't simply allow them to sit and rot while he went about his life. She thought, *"This is no ordinary guy. He could've given me up long ago, but he hasn't. Not only that, but he's also fine as hell sweet Jesus…"*

She felt at ease in his presence and was finally beginning to trust in him. She relaxed while watching him and her son play. He noticed her admiring him. He saw a glimmer deep within her gaze that piqued his interest.

For a brief moment, they zoned out Patrick Louis. She lowered her head, and their lips slightly touched. The warmth of her lips and the sweetness of her tongue made him want more. They kissed again. He reached for her and pulled her closer to him and they continued to share a passionate kiss. Patrick Louis jumped on them unexpectedly interrupting the intimate moment. They burst into laughter. They played together until his nap time.

CHAPTER FOUR

Santiago was sitting at his desk working when his mother entered his office. Because of their strained relationship, he hadn't spent much time with his parents. He only spent enough time with them when he wanted to know their progress in trying to track Amber. He looked up from his computer, unsure of why she was there. "Hello Mother," he said in a dry tone. He stood to his feet out of respect and helped her to her seat.

"What brings you by?"

"I was visiting your father's office. I needed to pick up some files for Ana." He was disgusted that she was still being controlled by Ana Maria and it showed on his face.

"Okay, so what do you want with me?"

"I stopped by to speak to you."

"Well, as you can see, I'm swamped with work, so you'll need to be brief.

"I'll be brief. Son, about a year or so ago, you promised me that you would find this girl and bring her to me, which hasn't happened. Can you tell me how that's going?"

"Mom, I haven't had much time to deal with that. I have my own issues plus my work, so I guess to answer your question I haven't had any luck finding her." She looked at him and went silent. He could tell something was bothering her.

"Why are you looking at me like that?"

"For the past few months, I've followed you. I was missing you because you stopped coming around. I wanted to know that you were okay. But anyway, I noticed that you're seeing a young girl with a child, which got me thinking: Why can't we seem to find this young lady and her child? For almost two years now we've not even heard so much as a peep from her. That's highly unlikely unless she's dead. We left no stone unturned and still no girl, so imagine my surprise when I followed you, only to find out you're seeing a young lady with a child that would be around the age of Ana's grandchild. She lives a few blocks from Ana. Wouldn't it be something if you've hidden the girl right in our faces?"

"So, you followed me? You're so dedicated to Mrs. Delgado that you would turn against me to help her. I never thought I would see the day. I should've known when you assaulted me for having my opinion you were mad, but now you're over the top. Are you insane? My own mother is brainwashed. What kind of hold does that woman have over you? And not only you, but Father too."

"Son, listen to me. I only want the girl and the baby. This has nothing to do with you. I love you, and I always will, but I love Ana too, and I want to help her."

"By destroying the lives of two people, right?"

"By giving Ana what's rightfully hers. Son, you're not a mother or a grandmother, so you don't know what the pain feels like not to have your family. You don't know what Ana is going through. She's aching, and this child is her last hope. It's her right as a grandmother." With a frown, he desperately tried to reach his mother one last time by pleading Amber's case.

"What about the rights of the mother? Does that matter to you at all? What if someone had done that very thing to you? Would you still think what you're doing is right?"

"Son, all I want is the girl and the baby. We can work out any issues between us. To be honest with you, I don't have to ask your permission because I can send someone over to get her, but I wanted to talk with you before I did."

"Would it matter to you if I told you I'm in love with her, and I love the child, and I can make a better life for him? For the first time in my life, I'm truly in love, and Mom she is magnificent. If you turn her over, you may as well kill me right along with her because I'm a dead man without her."

His mother noticed the desperation. Feeling somewhat betrayed, she was disappointed with him. With him protecting Amber, she realized that he'd gotten in way too deep. Too deep for her to save him, especially if Ana Maria were to find out. Thinking about his actions' implications, she felt he was putting her in a very awkward and dangerous position. She loved Ana Maria, and she never considered not turning the girl over to her. She saw things from her perspective, and as a close friend, she wanted to do what any sister would do. Isabella was disappointed in her son, so she didn't say anything to him. She got up from her seat and said, "I want to meet her. Take me to her now."

He tried to figure out her angle. He knew she already knew where Amber was, and he was quite sure she was being watched, so warning her would be of no use.

"If you harm her, if she dies, you'll never see me again because I'll take that to mean that you chose Mrs. Delgado over me. Is that understood?" She did not answer. He left his seat and cleared his desk. He got his keys and helped his mother to his car. They made the drive over to Amber's place. He let himself in with his keys. His mother was behind him. Amber was holding her son because she had just bathed him. She looked at Santiago. She looked at his mother and said, "What is this, Santiago?" Before he could tell her, Isabella walked over to her and extended her hand to her.

"I'm Isabella Burkett, Santiago's mother."

Amber recognized his mother. She was alarmed and she was very frightened. She looked at Santiago, confused and scared.

"What's going on?" He went over to Amber and the baby. He began explaining,

"Mother has been following me, and she found out about this place. She figured out that I was protecting you." His mother interrupted him,

"Ana Maria Delgado has been my friend and sister since childhood. We share an unbreakable bond. My friend has lost her two sons. When they died, the light in her eyes had dimmed. She's lost, and she's very lonely. Her only hope is her grandson. If I could give her that gift, her life would change for the better. My son was supposed to find you and bring you to me, but he disobeyed my orders. He's come to your defense. I told him that this situation wasn't about him but about getting Ana's grandchild to her. My son informed me that he's grown quite fond of you and he's in love with you. He wants to raise your child as his own. I wanted to meet you for myself. I can't remember my boy ever feeling this way about anyone." She produced a warm smile, studying the toddler while he sat with his mother.

Patrick reached for Santiago. With a head full of thick curly hair, the cutest smile, and widened light brown eyes that danced playfully from his mother to Santiago, he insisted on going over to Santiago. He walked over and took the baby, and held him close, and they played briefly. He only had on his training underwear. His little meaty thighs and baby belly were exposed.

"Come on, Patrick. Let's put on your clothes so that we can watch your favorite show, okay?" Santiago said.

Excited about the show, Patrick Louis clapped his hands and started singing one of his favorite songs. Santiago sang along with him as he got him dressed. While he was playing with the child, his mother was watching them closely while talking to Amber. With the looming chance that her son would disown her, she sought to try to find out more about the girl. Still, she intended to turn her over regardless of Santiago's threat. She visited with her alone so she could get to know her better. She needed to see what her son saw in her. Amber was careful not to overshare with her. She didn't speak of her parents or other family members, but she expressed her love for her son, which was evident.

"So, what do you have planned for your son's future?"

"I want him to live his dreams. Anything that he shows interest in doing, I'll do my best to make a way for him to succeed. I will be here for him whether he wants to attend college or pursue other goals. What I can tell you is that upon learning what his biological father went through, I wouldn't wish that on anybody. I understand that your friend wants my son. She wants to raise him in the organization. I love my son, and the thought of him living his life being hated or hunted by the police, FBI, and other criminals just doesn't sit well with me. I couldn't see my sweet innocent son being forced to take another man's life. Another mother would have to bury her child because of my son. No mother should want that for her child or any other mother's child, regardless of their relationship. As adults, we have responsibilities to ensure our children live a wonderful and peaceful life. They should be rooted and grounded in faith. They should be raised to be upstanding members of society and wonderful mentors to other young men and women. We shouldn't raise them to be criminals.

Santiago told me how grateful he was to you for allowing him to follow his dreams. He wants to live freely. We're not all cut from the same cloth. Just because I want to be an attorney or a doctor doesn't mean I should force that on my son. If I choose to build a criminal empire, I shouldn't want to involve my children. That would be totally irresponsible of me as a parent. Don't you agree?"

Isabella leaned back in her seat. She watched as her son played with the child. She looked back at Amber with a somber expression. Her eyes began to water.

"As the mother of a son, I definitely understand your concern." While she was talking to Amber, Patrick Louis ran to his mother. Amber gave him a stuffed toy. He was in a playful and exploratory mood. He took the toy to Isabella and began rambling to her in toddler language. She played with him for a few minutes. She picked him up and sat him on her lap. She smiled as he sang and clapped. He reminded her of Andre. Out of love for Ana Maria, she held him close to her heart. She wished Ana Maria could have this experience. She knew it would bring new life and great joy to her friend. She studied his face carefully.

"He's such a sweet little boy," she said.

"He's so friendly and handsome, too." Santiago took the baby to give his mother a break. She looked at Amber and smiled. Standing to her feet, she said,

"Son, please take me back to my car. It was very nice meeting you, dear. I see why my boy likes you. I'm sorry for all the trouble I've caused. I want you to know it's not me who wants to harm you. I want what's best for all involved, and it seems as if you and Santiago are doing what you feel is best for the baby. A child needs his mother. Enjoy your life. I'll figure something out. Son, let's go."

Santiago took his mother back to the office. They discussed Amber and the baby and their plan to further stall Ana Maria.

"So, I see why you like her. She has a good head on her shoulders. Her child is such an adorable little guy. I know Ana Maria would love to meet him. I wish she could, but as a mother, I can see her point, and I can also see my friend's point. I know she needs this child in her life, but the child doesn't need her. This is an extremely difficult decision for me to make, but I know all too well what a life of crime does to a child. That's why I sent you away. I wanted to protect you from this lifestyle. I know you witnessed me and your father's crimes, and I'm sorry for the things you've had to see. I saw how it affected you. It broke my heart, but we did what we had to do. I can honestly tell you that I won't allow that to happen to the child. I'm not going to mention I know anything about him.

But that poor girl has been on the run and locked up for a while now. They're practically in prison. We're going to have to do something about that. That poor child needs to run around free and not cooped up in that house. He needs to interact with other children. Isabella went on and on about how she wanted to help with the baby. Santiago began to witness a positive transformation in his mother. He pulled into the parking lot of the law firm. He walked over to his mother's side of the vehicle and helped her out of the car. She stood looking at him face to face.

"Son, I'll help you with anything you need. I won't turn her over to Ana. I want you to be happy." He leaned forward and kissed her on the cheek.

"Thank you, Mother." While they were doing that, Amber called Cindy and told her everything that happened.

"So, you mean to tell me that she followed him?" Cindy asked.

"Yes, and she had him bring her here. She visited with us for a while. She met my son. When she left, she apologized and spoke as though she was going to keep our secret. I can't be too sure, but I figured she would've brought Ana Maria with her without bringing Santiago if she was going to turn us over to her."

"So, you and Santiago are seeing each other?"

"We've become very close the past couple of years. He's the only man I'm really allowed to see. We haven't talked about a relationship or anything, but I can tell there is something special between us."

"Well, I don't know what to make of a future with you and him because of his father. He's still under Ana Maria's thumb. I'll say watch yourself, and if you ever want to try to go on your own again, we can always call Jessica Barnes or our contacts at the police department. So, let me know. At this point, I don't have any other advice for you. I just hope you stay safe. Keep your eyes open. I believe it's only a matter of time before Ana Maria finds you, but I'm going to follow your lead on this. Have you spoken with your parents this week?"

"Yes, I have. They're doing great at the safe house. They look good from what I see from our video chats. It's still too dangerous for us to meet up, but if God is willing, it'll be soon. I'm tired of hiding, but I'll hide forever to protect my child."

"Kiss him for me."

"I will."

"I love you, cousin. I'll call you next week."

"I love you too.", Blaine,

Cindy ended her call. She called a close friend, private detective Jessica Barnes. Her boyfriend Blaine works for her part-time as an investigator. Cindy wanted to inform her of Amber's situation. Jessica was sitting behind the wheel of a black Toyota in the parking lot of an apartment complex. An insurance company hired her to watch a client they suspected of insurance fraud. She didn't bring any food, so she stopped by the nearest truck stop in Benton and got a bag of Funyuns, a Little Debbie snack cake, and a Nehi peach soda, which she was snacking on when Cindy called.

"Jessie, what are you up to?"

"Hi Cindy; I'm just watching a subject for a client."

"Sounds like fun," Cindy said.

"Yeah, she's an easy target. She claims she hurt herself on the job. She leaves work early every day to visit her lover. He's a physical therapist. She's supposed to be in therapy at his place of business, but they've been meeting at his apartment every day. I guess he's in there giving her his own form of physical therapy. He'll go on billing her employer's insurance for his work. He seems to think she'll never recover from her so-called injuries. I suppose not, since he's in there blowing her back out every day. Oh, and did I forget to mention she's married?"

"Ooh girl, you get all the good cases," Cindy said.

"Nah, all of my investigators are on other assignments, so I decided to go ahead and work on this one myself. It's an easy one. Open and shut. A few pictures here and there and I'll be done. She's so stupid and careless; she makes this an easy job. So, what's up Cindy?"

"It's Amber. Santiago's mother, Isabella Burkett, showed up on her doorstep today."

"Is she cool?"

"She's okay for now. Mrs. Burkett had been following him, and she discovered he was hiding Amber. According to Amber, the woman wants to assist her and not turn her over to Ana Maria."

"So why don't we just hide her again?"

"We tried that once, but Santiago found her and since Ana Maria has so many people in her pocket, it's hard to trust anyone. She feels she's safer taking her chances with them."

"That's not good. People should be able to feel safe without having to worry about threats. They ought to be able to go to the police for help and not have someone who's secretly working for criminals betray the public's trust, but it happens. She's been on the run with that baby for two years now. There ought to be something we can do."

"Yes, my aunt and uncle were uprooted from their home as well. They, too, were forced into hiding. They can barely have contact with each other. They haven't even seen the baby in almost a year and a half. I must stay away because I'm the link to the whole case. I'm being watched, I think my phones are tapped. I have to talk to them on our burner phones. It feels so frustrating. I just want to let you know what's going on. Perhaps between you, me, and Blaine, we can come up with another plan to help them."

"Let me think of something. Also, I need to contact a few more friends and I'll get back to you. In the meantime, keep on doing what you're doing. I love you girl. We're not going to let anything happen to your cousin."

"I love you too."

Cindy ended the call. She sat for a while thinking of ways she could get to Ana Maria and kill her, but her security was tighter than that of the President. With bulletproof cars and heavily armed security, she didn't stand a chance.

CHAPTER FIVE

Ana Maria was down in the basement of one of her vacant properties in North Little Rock with Isabella standing by her side. They were there with three of her gunmen. Isabella dreaded being there because she knew another murder was about to take place. It was nine o'clock on a Sunday and already they had killed at least six people within the last two days who had managed to cross Ana Maria in some way or another.

The body count had become so high, that a record number of Arkansans were being reported missing weekly. The blood-thirsty matriarch couldn't seem to get enough of killing. The more she killed, the more senile she became to the point of talking to herself. Isabella found her behavior a bit disturbing. Ana Maria's latest murders were becoming increasingly serial in nature, and she seemed to be enjoying every minute of it. They were now about to commit two more murders.

Sitting before them were two young Caucasian men. One was a seventeen-year high school dropout. The other was his friend who was twenty-two years old. They were involved in an accident that cost the life of the nephew of Ana Maria's friend who happened to work for her. The older one, Brad, had been drinking at a party when he saw Josh. He stopped to give him a ride. Brad began texting his friends to see where the next party was so they could attend. He lost control of his vehicle and slammed head-on into oncoming traffic killing the associate. These young men left the scene of the accident instead of rendering aid or calling for help. Because they left the scene leaving him on the side of the road, the victim died from his injuries. After a brief search by the police, the boys were quickly arrested and were currently out on bail.

Ana Maria had them picked up and brought to her. Her men lured them to the home on the pretense of an employment opportunity paying them upfront to ensure they would come. When they arrived, they were immediately subdued. Ana Maria stood before them and began to speak.

"Do you know who I am?" she asked the frightened young men. They both shook their heads violently. Beads of sweat were pouring from Josh's head causing his dark hair to stick against his forehead. He tried to speak through the duct tape that was strapped tightly over his mouth filling his cheeks with air. He continued to try to plead for his life, but his voice was muffled.

"I'm Ana Maria Delgado." When they heard her announce her name, they knew they were going to die.

"You two were involved in an accident that killed someone very close to me. You were so heartless and cold that you allowed him to die on the side of the road instead of getting help for him, all because you were trying to avoid a DUI charge. What kind of cowardly shit is that? Because of you, I have to watch the friends I love suffer. This young man was a very valuable member of our organization. He was strategically put in place where we could take advantage of certain loopholes in the law. His involvement brought in millions of dollars for us. Now he's gone and I'll no longer be able to profit due to this loss. Here's what I want you two to know; when you hurt my people and my business, you're hurting me, and I don't like it."

Ana Maria put on a protective covering and gloves with Isabella's assistance. She retrieved her weapon from her handbag and handed her bag to Isabella to hold until she could complete her dirty deed. She walked up to Brad. She took one step and fired with a double tap to the temple. His head slumped down with blood and brain matter dripping and pooling in his lap and onto the floor. The seventeen-year-old who witnessed the death of his friend realized his fate and once again tried to plead for his life. He closed his eyes before she got close to him begging for his life. She turned her attention towards him and fired rapidly. Isabella, knowing how young the boy was, turned her head as Ana Maria cruelly emptied her gun into the head of a pleading teenage boy. A boy who ran with an older guy whose crime of covering up an accident had brought him to the end of his life.

Perhaps he felt compelled to cover up the crime by being coerced by his older companion with the possibility of threats or intimidation. Either way, he wouldn't get a second chance in life. He met his judge, jury, and executioner.

This wasn't the youngest person to be killed by Ana Maria. She was responsible for the deaths of hundreds of children who were caught in the crossfire of her killing sprees. Witnessing these deaths hit Isabella hard. She thought of her son when he was that age, young and immature. What if someone would've killed him?

She began to realize just how much she had allowed Ana Maria and her lifestyle to influence her over the years. Because of her love and longtime association with her, she had blindly followed her into killing innocent people all over the world, not once stopping to question her about what they were doing.

She trusted her from their youth, and because she'd saved her life and rescued her many times, she felt she owed her life to her. The problem for Isabella was that the older they got, the more evil Ana Maria seemed to become, especially after the deaths of her sons.

She watched as she placed her gun inside her designer handbag, not even bothering to clean the blood from it. She took off the gloves and protective covering and laid them on the floor. She and Isabella were escorted to the waiting vehicle. Isabella looked back at the lifeless bodies of the two victims. She knew they would never be heard from again. Ana Maria had a way of making anyone disappear without a trace. Isabella stepped into the car, this time a changed woman. For the first time in years, she questioned their friendship and her involvement with Ana Maria. She was growing tired of the senseless murders. She understood there were always causalities during any war, especially when you have as many enemies as Ana Maria Delgado, but to get involved in the deliberate killing of a seventeen-year-old was stretching it, especially for a woman of Ana Maria's standards.

Isabella felt that such a killing should've been beneath her, but because of her thirst for blood, she took it upon herself to murder the young men. Isabella stared out the window as the car slowly crept down Fairway and onto North Hills Boulevard. They were heading to the airfield adjacent to the Clinton National Airport. Ana Maria had a private jet waiting to take them to Miami to play their monthly card game with the rest of her friends from Los Zorros Blancos. With chatty laughter, she expressed the excitement about her trip back home as if she hadn't just killed two young men at point-blank range.

Santiago's voice played through Isabella's head. He was right. She lived her life in the shadows of Ana Maria's. She thought of how disgusted Santiago was with her due to her loyalty to her. She couldn't get her son's look of disapproval from her mind. She wanted him to love, respect, and honor her as his mother. Hearing him speak of how she and her husband had devastated his life broke her heart. She tried her best to shield him from her criminal activities, but she finally saw she wasn't as successful as she thought. She tried to put it out of her mind, but she couldn't, and it was breaking her heart. Her thoughts went to Ana Maria's grandson. She knew she had to protect him, especially since she hadn't protected her own son as thoroughly as she'd hoped. She was all the more adamant about helping to shield the child from the clutches of his ruthless grandmother.

Isabella wanted to slow down but Ana Maria was alone. She had no other family so she offered a large sum of money to whoever could find the child. Isabella was anxious to get with Santiago so that they could devise a plan to ensure Amber and her son's safety.

Close Call

Amber wanted to get out of the house for a while. She begged Santiago to take her and Patrick for a walk. He got the stroller while she bundled the tot in his coat and mittens, and they went for a stroll around the neighborhood. Normally, she would do her daily walk early in the morning, but she wanted to enjoy the brisk winter air, and she didn't want to be cooped up in the house for the rest of the day. They toured the neighborhood for a few blocks being careful not to go near Ana Maria's street. After about twenty minutes in, Patrick began to get a little fussy, so they decided to take him home. On the way back a large black SUV pulled slowly alongside them. It immediately stopped. The passenger inside let the window down as she recognized Santiago. It was Ana Maria Delgado!

"Santiago, what are you doing in the neighborhood?" Trying to play it cool, he blocked Amber's face with his body. He lifted the lapel of his black fur shearling sheepskin coat, buttoned the top button, and stood directly in the window blocking Ana Maria's view. Amber turned her back to the vehicle in hopes she wouldn't recognize her. "I'm visiting a friend. We're just out for a walk."

"Who is your friend? Care to introduce me?"

"She needs to get home. Her child is a little upset. I think he's hungry." Amber quickly walked the baby away from the area while Santiago continued to stall the curious woman.

"Is that the young lady you told me about a while back?"

"Yes, ma'am."

"Why don't you bring her by for dinner sometime? I would love to meet her.

"I will but now I must help her to get her child inside," he said.

"Well, I must get going. Enjoy your day."

"You too Mrs. Delgado." He stepped away from the vehicle as it pulled away and headed in the opposite direction.

She let her window up, and Santiago caught up with Amber. They hurried to her place. She was spooked. Her heart was pounding out of her chest. Once they made it inside, she undressed her son and laid him down for his nap, and she began nervously pacing the floor.

"Oh my god, that couldn't have gone any worse even if I wanted it to," she said.

"Relax Amber. She doesn't suspect a thing. I told her about you when I first brought you here. She just thinks you're some young lady that I'm infatuated with. This is her first time seeing me over in this area after all this time. We don't have anything to worry about."

"I think it's time for us to leave here. I can't take any chances." He walked up to her and took her by both hands facing her.

"Amber, do you trust me?"

"Yes, I trust you but it's her that I don't trust."

"Do you honestly believe that I'm going to allow anything to happen to you and your son?"

"I know you want to believe that nothing will happen, but I can't afford that luxury; not when my life hangs in the balance."

"Amber, I don't know if you know this or not but I'm falling in love with you. I care about you and your son. You two are like family to me. I'll do anything within my power to protect both of you even if it means putting my life on the line. I started out doing this for my friend Andre and his son, but after spending this time with you and getting to know you, I can see why Andre fell in love with you. I didn't mean for it to happen and in some way, I feel that I may be crossing some sort of boundary, but Amber, I can't help it. So, you see I'll do whatever it takes to make sure you're okay. If you feel uncomfortable being here, we can move but I think it would be risky. Let's just give it a few days. I'll stop by and talk to her, you know, throw her off the trail once more, and that should buy us some more time."

"I'm prepared to do this for the long haul, but do you think I'm ever going to be free of this woman? I hate to sound cruel and harsh but it's getting a bit old sitting here waiting for her to die so that we can live."

"Better days are coming, Amber." She looked hopeless. He pulled her close and held her as she sobbed. He spent the night with her for her comfort.

THE CONFRONTATION

Isabella and Ana Maria were having tea and a light lunch at her place. Isabella noticed she seemed to be in a foul mood. She figured she was having a down day thinking about the death of her sons but that wasn't the case. She was getting suspicious because, after repeated invitations for Santiago and Amber to join her for dinner, he never allowed them to meet. Ana Maria loved Santiago as one of her own even though he wasn't as fond of her as she was of him. Isabella picked up a tortilla and took a bite. She looked at Ana Maria and asked,

"Is everything okay? You seem to be upset about something." She exhaled and said,

"Not really. I have a lot on my mind."

"Well, what's bothering you? Is it something I can help you with?"

"You know, Isabella, it's been two years now, and we haven't found the girl nor my grandchild. Nobody can seem to find her anywhere, not my guys or your husband. It's as though she doesn't exist. How do you hide a beautiful young lady and her child? I thought about that for a while then I noticed your son here in my neighborhood visiting a young lady who just so happens to have a young child. The more I ask him about her, the more evasive he becomes. It's as if he doesn't want me to meet her, but why? Is he hiding something from me? Perhaps something he doesn't want me to know. So, I decided to watch them for a while. I rarely see the girl come out of the house, but I often see our Santiago coming to and from her place. What do you know about this situation?"

"Well, I've met her a few times. She seems to be a nice young lady. She's definitely not the same girl we're looking for. I would have turned her over to you if she were, you know that.

She's just somebody he's been seeing you're making too much of this. This whole grandchild thing has taken a toll on you. You're becoming desperate. You're seeing things that aren't there and you're suspicious of everybody.

Why just the other day, when that car rushed around ours, you got so angry that you ordered your driver to pull alongside them. You were about to fire your weapon into the car until you realized it was a lady in labor with her husband and kids in the car. You've been making a lot of rash decisions lately and I'm getting a little concerned for you.

Santiago is young and he's always been a private person. Who knows why he does what he does? He may not be ready for her to meet everyone just yet. And besides, he may not be all that serious about her. Don't forget about the organization. We can't let everybody in on what we're doing. It will take a special type of girl to live in our family. Let him take this relationship at his own pace. When he's ready; he'll bring her to meet the family."

She let out a deep sigh. "I suppose you're right. I have been feeling a little beside myself lately. It's so difficult living alone. I get my hopes up for a possible grandchild and I can't seem to find the child anywhere. He's probably out there living his life without me."

"Maybe there is no child," Isabella said trying to steer her away from the idea, but she was holding on to hope.

"There has to be. She received money from my family, so even if she has no child, she needs to tell me where the money is."

"Well from what Santiago explained to us, Andre wanted the girl to have the money because he loved her. That was a gift from his heart and it's rightfully hers. She was only supposed to get the rest if there was a child involved. Maybe she lost the child, perhaps in a miscarriage. I mean, answer this question: what woman we

82

know will walk away from millions of dollars allotted to her for her child? The father is deceased, and she can have all that money. Remember she doesn't know you're looking for her. I think she may have lost the baby. I say any money that Andre gave her is hers to keep. Since he loved her, she should be allowed to live in peace. It's not like you need the money. Why not do as Anton did and fulfill his dying wish by helping his girlfriend? Who knows why he loved this girl? Maybe she stood by his side. Maybe she showed him her value, worth, and loyalty. There are so many variables. I think you need to sit back and take a long look at this. I also think you're starting to make a lot of mistakes; Mistakes that could come back to haunt us. You're leaving evidence of our business all over town. We've come too far from the slums in Havana to America, and we don't want to spend the rest of our lives in an American prison; well, at least I don't want to. I'd rather die first and I'm not ready to die, are you?"

"What more do I have to live for? My life is all but over. You're trying to tell me that I may not have a grandchild. You are saying that and it's like you're taking away my hope. Maybe that's why I'm making all these mistakes as you say. Maybe I just don't care anymore."

"Well, you should care. I think you should take some time away from the business to rest. We have everything we need. We have more money and power than anyone in this region. What else do you need?"

"I want someone to carry on the legacy of my father-in-law; someone who truly deserves it and will be as passionate as I was when Ernesto turned things over to me."

"Ana let's face it; it's over. Stop doing this to yourself. You'll have to come to the realization that there may be no baby. It's okay to grieve for your sons; that's a mother's right but you're losing it. All you talk about is this child. You need some rest or a vacation. You have trusted men under your reign; you should get one of them to take over the business for a while."

Ana Maria looked at her as if she didn't have a clue. "Isabella, I've fought long and hard to get to where I am today. I've created this empire. After my father-in-law died, my husband and I kept this business going; surely, I didn't do all of that just to turn it over to the hired help. If I choose to believe there is a grandchild out there, then afford me that luxury."

"Suit yourself, but you need to prepare to choose a successor to handle the business since it means so much to you. Everyone is not up for the challenge of doing the things we had to do to get where we are in life. We had to kill to survive. We had to fight our way out of many dangerous situations. As a result, we've created many enemies which we've had to eliminate.

I think somewhere along the lines we've forgotten that we don't have to fight as hard as we used to because we've just about eliminated all threats. The conflicts we have today are ones we've created ourselves. It's okay to not try to conquer everything or take over every organization. I mean we must ask ourselves, what's it all for? Why can't we be happy with what we already have?" Ana Maria said,

"I'm getting up in age but I'm not dead. I didn't work this hard to sit somewhere in the corner of a nursing home waiting to die. I'll remain on top, and I will die on top. No one will ever disrespect me or treat me as some old has-been. I'm not about to let these little young punks try to muscle their way in and take over an empire I built over a lifetime. I won't stand for it. That's why I must continue to kill these new-coming gangsters. They want my business and my connections. They try to drive a wedge between me and my business partners. I will fight until my dying breath to keep that from happening."

"You're addicted to power. It's because of the abuses you suffered at the hands of others. You feel that if you're powerful enough and if everyone fears you, you won't be abused or taken advantage of. You've built a wall around you so great that no one can get in or out. You have no tolerance for others, and if someone does the slightest thing to offend you, although innocent, you kill them.

These deaths over the past few years were senseless. You don't even give people options anymore. You see something you want, and you kill them and take it, and what for? Do you know how many lives we've impacted over the years? I stood with you when we were killing with a purpose, but now we're killing innocent people and I'm beginning to wonder about you. I've never questioned you and I've always stood by you, but this is becoming a bit overwhelming for me. I don't like harming innocent people."

Ana Maria listened carefully as her friend continued to be the voice of reason between them. She finally had enough and became defensive.

"Isabella, if it were not for me, we would've been murdered when we were teens. Have you forgotten about the rapes and murders of our friends? What about the deaths of our parents? The many atrocities we suffered at the hands of others. It was I who fought for us. It was because of my tactics that we survived. I'm the reason we were able to flee when Fidel Castro and his regime came into full power. I've carried both of us and this organization on my shoulders even before my father-in-law died.

My husband was no good. He couldn't be relied upon, and he couldn't be trusted. He put this entire organization and our boys at risk with his many whores and wild parties. Neither discretion nor fidelity was his greater qualities. While I was building this empire with my blood, sweat, and tears brick by brick, he was tearing it down. Whatever I accomplished he tried to destroy. He was out of control.

He went to the feds and sang like a bird. I could've handled all of that, but he had gone so far that my hands were tied. Now as much as I loved him, he became a liability to this family, so I had him assassinated. It had to be done for the sake of our children, my life, and yours, and especially the organization. He talked too damn much. I heard personal business that was strictly between us on the streets. Things others had no way of knowing unless he told them. How could I trust that he hadn't mentioned me to the feds? I couldn't let him continue putting us in jeopardy. We could've gotten the death penalty and who would've raised our kids?"

Isabella was alarmed that Ana Maria openly admitted to killing her own husband, but it made sense. Nobody knew he was going to Cuba but her. Hector happened to die on his first trip back there in years. As she sat and thought about it; it was clear that Ana Maria was involved. Hector wasn't a great man. He *was* foolish and shady in his business deals, and he *did* manage to bring a lot of unwanted attention to the family. That's why his father, Ernesto, trusted Ana Maria more than him.

She continued to let the news soak in about Hector's death. Immediately she began to worry about Santiago. If she killed her own husband, the father of her children, and the son of her beloved father-in-law Ernesto, then Santiago's life would be in danger for sure. Especially if she learned the truth that he was betraying her by keeping the child from her. She thought of her own life being in danger as well. She had to warn Santiago. She sat and ate lunch. She was worried. Her stomach was in knots, and she could no longer stomach her tea. After her lunch with Ana Maria, she left to find her son.

CHAPTER SIX

Walter Burkett was leaving the federal courthouse from the Ramone trial.

Francisco Ramone was one of many overseers of Ana Maria's financial business transactions. He had been on trial for his illegal business transactions within the company. He helped launder millions of dollars into other businesses that operated as fronts for the Delgado cartel and Walter Burkett's illegal income.

If his company was found guilty, he and his partners could've owed millions in fines and possible convictions that would've netted them years in prison. One of his top executives, who had been under investigation, turned whistleblower and promptly turned over a few files to the feds in return for leniency. Ana Maria and Walter paid to have him located. They killed him as well as a few other men hired to guard him until he could testify. They had his home bombed. The explosion was made to look like a gas leak.

The feds had a little evidence from the whistleblower, and they were promised more, but that evidence was destroyed in the fire. They still wanted to try Ramone based on what little evidence they had, which wasn't much, but they were hopeful that they could get a conviction.

Walter's visit to the federal judge was to ensure that even if his client were convicted, he would do no time. By the time his trial had come, the evidence had been so watered down that they found in favor of Francisco Ramone. They also concluded that Francisco was a victim of the whistleblower who sought to cover his crimes by blaming the defendant. He was found innocent and allowed to return to work. His name was cleared. Walter was on the phone with Ana Maria telling her the news. She breathed a sigh of relief and invited him and Isabella over for a celebration.

Francisco got into a separate vehicle, and Walter went to his law firm.

He noticed Isabella was there visiting Santiago's office. He could tell they were discussing something important by their hand gestures and posture. Isabella had already informed her son about Ana Maria's suspicions. He was alarmed. They were discussing what to do next. As they were talking, Walter walked in. Isabella stopped talking and looked at Walter. She tried to force a smile on her face, but he could tell something wasn't right.

"What's happening in here? Did somebody die, and you forgot to tell me?"

"Hello Walter, how was court today?"

"I won as usual. What's going on here?"

"Oh, it's nothing to be alarmed about; just a little girl-trouble. Our son here just needed some motherly advice. It's nothing serious." She stood to her feet to greet him. She kissed him on the lips.

"Congratulations, Walt. Wanna go and celebrate?" He loosened up and relaxed as she kissed him once more.

"Sure; Ana Maria invited us over for drinks tonight."

"Well, that sounds great. It's a date then," she said trying to divert his attention away from Santiago. Walter stared at him and asked,

"Son, are you sure you're okay?"

"Yes, Father, I'm okay."

"Well, if you need my advice, you know I'm here for you. Me and your mother have been married for close to forty years so you know I must be doing something right to keep this lovely lady around all these years."

"I'm alright, Father, trust me. Thank you. I have to get back to work. I'll see you later, Mother."

"I love you son." She walked Walter to his office, and they chatted and left together.

After discovering Ana Maria was a little suspicious, Santiago had Amber moved from the home to an apartment in Pine Bluff. After his parents left the office, he drove to where she was staying.

In the meantime, his parents were at Ana Maria's place having drinks and eating a meal prepared by her. She was upbeat and was glad the trial of her business partner was finally behind them. After a few drinks, she was feeling mellow as she had already begun to celebrate before they arrived. She told old jokes which they had all heard before while reminiscing about their younger days. She shared just about any and everything on her heart. Walter was feeling great, too, and they were happy they could continue their working relationship with Francisco Ramone. Walter said,

"Ana Maria; here's to millions already made in the past, and we're going to make millions more in the future. Congratulations," he said, lifting his glass for a toast.

"Salud! Congratulations to you, Burkett, for another job well done."

"Congratulations again dear," Isabella said. They continued eating their meal. Walter said,

"Ana, you really outdid yourself with this meal."

"Thank you, Walter, but my sister Isabella is a great cook also. I taught her everything I know." Isabella smiled and said,

"Yeah, but Walt and Santiago seem to enjoy eating here. You add that special touch from home to all your dishes. I can't quite get it right like you. I may be good but you're the best."

"Where's Santiago? It's a shame he's not here to celebrate his father's win in court and enjoy this nice meal. He loves it when I cook."

"He was at the office moping over some lady when I left," Walter said.

"Oh, is that the same little girl I've been asking him to bring by here?"

"I don't know," Walter said. "I didn't even know he was seeing anybody."

"Well, he's been seeing her for quite some time. She lives right around the corner. I saw them walking one evening when I was on my way home. He's never brought her by, so we could tell if she's good enough for him. Isabella says she's met her. Initially, I thought she was the young lady we were looking for with my grandchild, but Isabella says she's not. And to think I had them followed."

Walter was stunned at what she had just admitted. He looked at her with a raised brow,

"You had Santiago followed?"

"Yes, I was curious about this mystery girl he's seeing. Think about it; she does have a child around the same age as my grandchild. I thought she was the girl, and perhaps he was hiding her from me?"

"But why would you think that our son would do something like that of all people?" Walter asked, setting his drink down. He was confused and disturbed by her confession.

"I don't know, I guess I was curious. Isabella says he's just taking his time with this one to make sure she's the right one."

Walter thought about his son for a while. He was alarmed that Ana Maria actually had him followed. He was upset about the news. He thought, *"Why would Ana have my son followed and what was she going to do to him if her suspicions were true?"* Walter loved his son, and knowing she had him followed angered him. He looked at his wife with a slight frown aimed at his wife; he was upset she hadn't told him about Santiago dating the girl. He ate the rest of his dinner, but he didn't enjoy any of it. He could hardly wait until they got in the car so he could discuss the matter further. Once dinner was over, they said their goodbyes and left. Walter immediately snapped when they got in the car.

"Isabella dear, what in the hell is going on? Why is she having our son followed? Did you know about this?"

"Yes, I knew only after she told me."

"Oh, this is not good, honey. This means she doesn't trust him. She doesn't trust us after all we've done for her. How could she do this to us? If she would've found anything you know she wouldn't have hesitated to kill our son, right?"

"Yes, I know; that's why I diverted her attention away from him."

"So, this girl that he's seeing, who is she really?"

"I can't tell you?"

"What?! What do you mean you can't tell me? Is she the girl we've been looking for?"

"Walter, you know I don't like lying to you, so I'm going to let Santiago tell you."

"No, I need you to tell me." Isabella exhaled. She wouldn't give him an answer. He knew that meant Santiago was protecting the girl.

"Look, we've got to get our son out of this. Ana will kill him if she finds out he's been lying to her. We've got to turn the girl over to her. She's not our issue. That's between Ana and the girl. She can do what she sees fit with her, but I don't want my son involved in this."

"It's too late, Walter. Not only is he involved, but he's also in love with the girl. Ana is going to kill him even if he turns her and the child over. Not only will she kill him, but she'll also have to kill us too. She won't hesitate to do it. Did you know she confessed to me that she was the one who had her husband Hector killed? She usually tells me everything, but for years, I never knew she had him assassinated. She said it was because he went to the feds, and he put her and the kids in jeopardy. If she killed him, then you already know she won't have an issue with killing us. She'll feel we betrayed her. It's too late to tell her. We have to do what we can to protect Santiago."

"You get that boy on the phone right now! Call him Isabella; I'm not playing with you." She fumbled for her phone. She called, but she didn't get an answer. "He's not answering, dear."

"Walter sped to Santiago's place. He didn't see his car in the driveway. He called his phone and left an urgent message for him to call. When Santiago realized that he had multiple missed calls from his parents so late in the evening, he called them back.

"Hello, Dad?"

"Son, what's going on? Ana tells me that she had you followed because she thinks you have the girl we've been looking for. Do you know what you've done by doing this? You've put this entire family's life on the line by helping this girl."

"So, I guess Mother told you."

"She didn't have to tell me. It's what she didn't say and now you're confirming it. You would put our lives in jeopardy for this girl and this child. Why would you do this to us? What were you thinking?"

"Dad, I'm not like you and Mom. I can't sit around and watch innocent people die. Especially not an innocent mother and watch her child be taken away from her while she is senselessly murdered. What type of man do you think I am?"

"Son, you'll start a war if Ana finds out."

"She won't find out unless you tell her." There was temporary silence. Santiago was curious as to what his father was thinking.

"Father, you aren't going to tell her, *are* you?"

"Son, let me think. I'll call you later."

He ended the call and rubbed his forehead in frustration.

"Isabella, what are we going to do? Maybe I can get the girl and kill her and then hand the child over to Ana; that way, the girl won't tell her our son was involved in hiding her all this time."

"What will you tell your son? He's not going to stand by and let that happen. He would give his life for this girl. You don't know how much he loves her. He loves the child too, so yes, go ahead and kill the girl, and you'll lose your son in the process. With the pain and anger he'll feel over her death, he'll confront you as well as Ana, so either way, we're all dead. Now think of something else."

"I don't know what to do. We have to discuss this as a family," Walter said.

Walter expressed his feelings of frustration over Santiago's choice. *"Santiago, why did you have to get in the bed of the enemy out of all the women in this state?"* They continued on their route and finally made it home. Walter paced the floor all night until Isabella begged him to come to bed. After sleeping on the issue, he knew his only recourse was to protect his son which meant protecting Amber as well. He would die before he would allow Ana Maria to find out what Santiago had done. He called him over to their home. They discussed the matter over breakfast. Santiago saw the softness in his father's face and his concern over his involvement with Amber.

"Son, I sure hope you love this girl because you have traded her life for ours."

"Father, nobody has to die if you help me. I love her. She's incredible. I didn't set out to love her. I just wanted to prolong her life. Father, Andre cared about her, and that's why he left her the money. I simply carried out his wishes. I don't think he would've wanted his son to grow up with Mrs. Delgado because he didn't want to be in the business himself. His mother forced him. Andre was a great guy and a good friend. Even Anton opted to give the girl the money that Andre left for her as his brother's last wish. Once we both found out she was pregnant, Anton wanted to take care of her. When he died, I took up her cause. It seems the only person who wants this innocent mother dead is Mrs. Delgado so she can take the child and raise him the way she did the boys. They hated that lifestyle, and so did I.

Rather than being allowed to live my dreams, I'm forced to work at a law firm you built from a life of crime. I'm forced to work for you and your shady clients. I'm really good at what I do, and I can make a lot of money for many wealthy corporations, but you're holding me back. I can't take on my own clients because I'm bombarded with yours. I'm living your life, not my own. I can't even love the woman I want. This isn't living.

My life has been stolen from me, just like Anton and Andre's. You and Mother have managed to live your lives and pursue your goals, but I feel like I'm living my life in a bubble, and I hate it."

Walter looked into his son's eyes. He could see the pain on his face. The pain he'd caused with his criminal lifestyle. He didn't want him in the criminal business, yet he forced him to handle all the accounts of his criminal clientele. The truth is that Santiago is the only person he truly trusts. Out of respect and honor for his father, Santiago fell in line.

"Son, I'm sorry. I had no idea what this was doing to you. I don't want you to hate us. I just thought that since we're a family, you know..."

"I love you and Mother. I've been made to feel awkward because I'm not cruel and heartless. You two can't seem to decide if you want me to be a criminal or a saint. I don't want anything to do with the business, and to tell you the truth, I don't understand why you two are so deep into it. We have more money and influence than anybody in this state. It's a shame that our name has got to be synonymous with the Delgado cartel and other corrupt names. Whenever someone hears my last name; it automatically strikes fear in their hearts. They know I'm your son, and they fear me because of it. I don't want to be known as a criminal. That's not me. I want to make something of my life. It's a father's dream to have his son carry on his name or to be like him, but father, ask yourself, do you want me to be like you? If I had sons, would you want us all to follow in your footsteps? If you wanted me to be a criminal, you should've kept me here and broken my spirit the same way Mrs. Delgado broke my friends. They hated what their mother did to them. They turned out to be ruthless killers, but they were a product of their environment. I don't want that for her grandchild, and you know that's her plan. Can we spare that child the heartache and pain and give him a chance at a happy, normal life, Father?"

Walter stood with his hands on his hips. One of the evilest men in the state of Arkansas thought about what his son was telling him. Santiago's speech moved him. If it had been anyone else, he wouldn't have been as compassionate, but this wasn't just anyone else. This was his son, his only child. The son of his true love. He walked over to Santiago and placed his arm around his shoulder.

"Son, let me take care of everything for you." Santiago hugged his father.

"Father, I want you to know that I love and respect you and Mother. I'm truly grateful for everything you've done for me, but I don't feel as though I can fit into your lifestyle, and I pray that you respect my choice just as I respect you. Please don't ask me to turn my friend over to Mrs. Delgado. What purpose would it serve? Please don't allow anything to happen to her."

"I won't, son," His father said.

They sat together and discussed what to do next. Walter thought that perhaps Santiago and Amber should leave town for a while and tell Ana Maria that he was leaving town to open his own practice elsewhere. They came up with the plan to tell her that Santiago and the girl ended the relationship, and she went back to her child's father and that Santiago would move away for a fresh start. Over the next few weeks, Santiago and his father grew closer than ever.

Walter began to rethink his position in the criminal organization. Hearing his son speak of Ana Maria's boys weighed heavily on his mind. Just like Isabella, he, too, never considered what their actions did to the boys. As he sat at his desk, he thought about having grandchildren of his own. What type of legacy was he going to leave for them, especially if Santiago chose not to allow them in his kids' lives? What if he went to prison, or even worse, what if he was killed? He wondered what would happen to him and his wife if they continued their dirty deeds. He had many things to consider. All these years, he felt invincible.

He never considered that Ana Maria would think of turning on him and his family, especially with all they'd done and gone through together. He, too, was alarmed to hear that she killed her husband even though he knew she was capable of killing anyone. He now regrets the partnership because she knew so much about them. He treated her like family, so he hid nothing from her.

She knew his family, friends, and others he cared about, and he was sure she wouldn't hesitate to send him a message by harming those he loved if he dared cross her. But he was going to protect his family and his interests at all costs. He just needed to be sure that his wife was on board with him and that she was willing to break the close bond that she and Ana Maria shared to protect their own. He needed a total commitment from her.

Once he felt he had her on board, he was convinced he would devise a great plan. If all else failed, he would kill Ana Maria himself. Isabella and Walter loved her dearly. Killing her would be equivalent to killing his blood-born sister, and for that reason, they were hesitant to kill her immediately. If it were anyone else, there would be no hesitation in eliminating the threat. They would only spare her life if they could be convinced that she wouldn't hurt Santiago.

CHAPTER SEVEN

Ana Maria hadn't been feeling well. She was often tired and restless. At Isabella's urging, she had her doctor give her a thorough examination. She was diabetic and had high blood pressure as well as some minor heart problems due to her age and the stress of the loss of her children. Not being able to locate her grandchild was taking its toll on her physically and mentally. Her doctor suggested that she see a grief counselor to properly deal with her mental health issues.

She decided she was about ready to retire. She'd conquered most of her enemies, but she still felt she had one more mission to complete: kill Cindy Brooks for the death of Anton. It was early in the morning, and she was lounging around in her bedroom. She began reading over the police report. Timing was everything to Ana Maria. If she moved too soon, she knew she would be blamed. Enough time had passed, and she was finally ready.

She carefully studied the report and each witness' account of the shooting incident. She began creating her list, taking note of officials and the prosecutor who refused to prosecute Cindy. She also took the names of all the witnesses and those involved in the case. The names that were added to her hit list were Cindy, her boyfriend, Blaine Cooper, her friends Jessica Barnes and Daniel Clark, also known as Big Dan, and lastly, Amber Brooks. The very girl she was looking for had her grandchild. She looked closer at the report. She hadn't noticed Amber's name before. She couldn't believe she'd overlooked it. She was alarmed that Amber was there. Not only was she there, but she was also actually involved in the melee. She admitted to killing several men in self-defense, and she wasn't charged either. That bit of news was very interesting to her. Now, she had just cause to kill Amber. She quickly called

Walter and demanded that he come over. She also called Isabella, who hitched a ride with her husband to her place.

When they arrived, Ana Maria was pacing the floor and fuming with heated rage. She was clearly upset. She dropped the police report on her dining-room table. They gathered around for a seat.

"Burkett, take a look at this report and tell me what you see."

He briefly scanned the documents. She waited impatiently for him to notice what she'd found. After a few seconds, he shifted his eyes to Ana Maria, confused about what he was supposed to be seeing.

"What is it, Ana?" With one hand on her hip and the other pointing violently at the report, she said,

"Take a look at the names on the report." He looked over all the names and made a mental note. The last name would haunt him. It was Amber Brooks. He tried to pretend he didn't understand, but he instantly made the connection. Amber was there when Anton was killed. She was pregnant and taken to the hospital, where she recovered from minor injuries.

"Ana, we've gone over this report a thousand times; what are you seeing that I'm not seeing?"

"Oh, come on, Burkett, you tell me you don't see that girl's name on the report, the same girl who was pregnant by my son. The one we're looking for. She was a part of this whole thing. She was involved in the killing of my son. Hell, for all I know, she may have had Andre murdered too. I want her found. I need answers. She gets pregnant by my son, he dies, and she collects the money. Later, she's in the same place when his brother is murdered; not only that, she admitted to shooting some of my men in self-defense.

Something's not right about this Burkett. Where's the damn girl? I want you to find her, turn over every stone in this county and this state; hell, turn over every stone in this country, but I need her found."

Isabella gripped her chest. She was afraid for Santiago for sure. She knew if they were found, Amber was going to die. By Ana Maria's account, Amber wasn't an innocent mother looking to protect her son; she was actively involved in the death of one brother and the suspicious unsolved death of the other. Even Isabella wanted to know more about her. She wanted to know if her own son's life was in jeopardy. She knew nothing about Amber, and she only hoped that Santiago was safe and wouldn't end up dead like Ana Maria's boys. She needed to talk to the girl herself. She was upset. She stood to her feet and said, "I think I'm going to be sick." She made her way to the nearest bathroom. She puked her breakfast.

Afterwards, she washed her face. Ana Maria thought she was upset on her behalf. She went back to sit with her husband. After she laid out her plans to attack the prosecuting attorney and Cindy, she began making plans to retaliate against everyone else on her hit list. She felt her life had new meaning. She thrived on trouble, and somehow, it excited her. The more she killed, the better she felt. It was an addiction. After she gave Walter his orders, she got a shot of tequila and sat back, thinking of how it would feel to have all of her enemies dead.

She wanted to kill Amber and Cindy with a prized weapon she'd owned since she was seventeen. The one she used to commit her first murder-for-hire. She finally had it engraved with the words *"Beautiful Assassin."* Murders committed with this gun were personal in nature.

To her, these deaths would signify a badge of honor and a special retirement gift to herself from the criminal organization, thereby ending her reign. She was ready to rest and either enjoy life with her grandchild or die in peace.

Isabella and Walter were in the car together. She addressed her concerns to him.

"Walter, did you know that the girl that Santiago is with was the same girl at the house when Anton was killed?"

"No, I honestly never actually put it together. Things were happening so fast, and we've been busy doing a million other things. I can hardly keep up with my own business, let alone Ana Maria's and the rest of her crew."

"I'm concerned about our son, dear. This girl may not be as innocent as she seems. I mean, she was Andre's girlfriend; he ends up dead, and nobody knows why, then she gets money from his estate, and she disappears. Our son gave her that money and now he's with her and claiming he's in love with her. She may be deceiving him. You know how gullible he can be at times, especially where women are concerned. Whatever she's hiding, I'll find out because if she hurts my child, she won't have to worry about Ana Maria because I'll kill her myself."

"Do what you feel you have to Isabella. It does look mighty suspicious of her. Let's talk to him. Don't tell him of our suspicions. Let's all talk together. If something doesn't add up, you kill her. Santiago will be upset but when it comes down to his safety, we will do what we must."

Isabella called Santiago and asked him to come over later that evening. He went to visit. He trusted that his parents had his best interest in mind. He hugged his mother as he walked in the door. He spoke to his father. Because the relationship was no longer strained, he didn't have to force himself to be kind. They shared a little small talk. Isabella sat him down and began discussing what Ana Maria told them but not everything.

"Son, I need to let you know something. Ana Maria's at it again. She called us over for a meeting. She's looking for the girl." His father interrupted, "Yeah she seemed to be even more upset and more eager to find her."

"Son, what do you know about this girl other than she is Andre's ex-girlfriend and the mother of his child?" his mother asked.

"I know she's sweet, kind, and genuine."

"Un huh, so did you know her before Andre died?"

"No, Mother, I knew nothing about her until after his death. Anton invited her to my office for the distribution of the will. It was then we discovered she was pregnant. How many times do I have to go over this with you?"

"I'm just asking. Do you trust her?"

"Sure, I do mother. Why do you ask?"

"Because if we're going to put our lives on the line to help her, I want to know that she's worth it. We have to hide her and the child quickly because Ana is pulling out the heavy artillery for this one. A lot of people are about to be killed over the next few months, and if she finds you with the girl and realizes we're helping her, we will all be killed."

"What do you suppose we do, Mother?"

"Let's go and visit with Amber as a family."

Isabella wanted to talk to Amber. If she didn't get the right answers from her, she was prepared to kill her immediately, regardless of how Santiago felt. He was a little afraid but trusted that his mother wouldn't do anything. He took his parents to where Amber was staying. She was afraid when she saw Walter coming in with them. She immediately ran to pick up her son. Santiago said,

"Don't be alarmed, Amber. They're here to help. We can't continue to do this alone. You can trust them."

Amber was reluctant to trust them, especially Walter. He helped his mother with her jacket. They were seated. His father introduced himself, but she already knew who he was, and she was very afraid. Directing his conversation towards Amber, he began to speak,

"Amber, we're here because we need a few answers from you. My son loves you, and he says he trusts you, but I'm having a few issues with that. Hear me out."

Santiago took his place by Amber and the child. With a guarded posture, he shielded Amber. They listened as his father continued.

"Isabella and I were under the impression that you're an innocent victim and we were prepared to offer you our full support at our son's word, but something's not adding up with you. You were dating Andre Delgado. He was murdered, and nobody knows who did it. You received three million dollars from his estate. Afterwards, Anton was killed in his home, and we discover that you were there. Not only were you there, but according to the police report, you helped kill a lot of people within the Delgado organization.

Nobody's heard from you until you showed up being protected by my son. I need to know what kind of game you're playing. Explain yourself, please?"

Santiago was curious about the information he had just learned from his father. He wanted to know the truth from Amber. He waited anxiously to hear what she had to say. Amber trembled. She began to speak.

"The night Andre died, I was at the cabin in Russellville. We were all on the run because of the war between the Delgados, and Cassias White's men. They killed a lot of Anton's people. They were bombing the clubs in Miami and most of their businesses. Anton was on the run, and Andre forced me to go along instead of allowing me to return home to my own family. The night Andre died, he said he had some business to attend to, so he made me stay at the cabin, and he left. I went to bed. I was awakened by Anton and his men informing me that Andre had been killed. I was allowed to go home the following day.

I heard from Anton a month later telling me about the money. I was just as surprised as anyone else. At the reading of the will, I was told about the baby clause. I told them about my pregnancy. I wasn't going to mention it on the advice of my cousin. She was afraid that Anton would take my baby. I was told I would get an inheritance for my baby. I felt I owed it to him to receive all that his father wanted him to have. Anton took me in, and he took care of me. He said he wanted the baby to be healthy. I trusted him.

One evening, he took me to his home, where he had been drinking. He violently raped me throughout the night. He was angry with my cousin Cindy. The sexual assault was another way to get back at her, so he recorded the rape and used the incident to taunt her. He then sent for her so he could kill her. When she arrived, he instructed a female employee to take her out back and kill her. When she realized our lives were in danger, she fought back. There was a violent gun battle. I did what I had to do to survive. Cindy shot Anton, and he died that day. That's the truth. I didn't know Andre and Cindy knew each other until we all met up one day by happenstance. She was against the relationship from the beginning, but I ignored her repeated warnings. Now, here I am, hiding out because I refused to listen. Yes, it's true that I was in Anton's home the day he was killed, but it was because he brought me there under the guise of taking care of me and the

104

baby; I didn't think he would sexually assault me. The police have the video of the assault."

"So, you're saying you're an innocent victim in this whole thing," Isabella asked, her arms folded. She listened carefully to every detail of the story.

"Mrs. Burkett, have you ever made a decision in life that you wholeheartedly regretted? I regret ever going out with Andre Delgado. Had I known it would result in this much trouble, I would've declined his offer for dinner. The only good thing about the relationship is our son. Once Anton died, my cousin told me that it would be wise for me to leave town. She felt that Mrs. Delgado would come for the baby. I listened to her and left. Soon after, Santiago found me. I didn't seek out your son; he found me. He told me he was concerned for the baby and for my safety. That's why I'm here today."

"So, you were not part of a plan to kill the Delgado boys and take their money because that's what Ana is thinking, and quite frankly, it looks rather suspicious."

"Mrs. Burkett, I never would've thought in a million years that Andre would leave me any money. Our relationship wasn't even that serious. All I wanted was to have a little fun and go on a few shopping sprees. This fancy older guy was spoiling me and buying me nice things. We were traveling by private jet and doing things I never imagined. Cindy warned me to leave the relationship, but I was having fun. She continued her warnings, telling me they were criminals, but I didn't believe her. Not until I noticed suspicious activities and saw news stories about the Delgados. I realized how deeply they were rooted in crime. By then, it was too late, and I was caught up. I wasn't allowed to leave.

When everyone around Andre began dying, he became very emotional, clingy, and unstable. He requested that I have his child.

Reluctantly, I did. I never thought that a little fun would turn into me having my family uprooted and being on the run with my son. What good is having money when you can't even enjoy it? I miss my parents, my school, and my friends. I want my life back. I don't give a damn about that money. It's evil. It has cost me nothing but pain.

Look at my son. He doesn't know what it means to interact with other children because he always has to stay cooped up with his mommy. He can't roam around and play in the sun because he's always covered up. No, ma'am, this is not the life I signed up for. I was just a silly girl with silly dreams, and I was having such a good time that I never stopped to think of the consequences. I should've stayed in law school instead of thinking about men. I wish I had listened to Cindy and my parents."

Walter was sitting, watching her carefully while taking in her story. For the most part, he believed her, but he still wanted her to convince him further because he was prepared to kill her if need be. He said,

"The way you present the story; it appears it was all in self-defense."

"Mr. Burkett, there was an undercover FBI agent in the room who witnessed the entire scene. Everything happened just as I told you. I'm not smart enough to be a part of some elaborate scheme to kill drug lords and take their money. Are you serious? I'm just a country girl. My folks are from Union County, Eldorado, Arkansas. It's comical to think I could even come up with something like that. I just want my life back and my freedom."

Amber began to sob. Santiago pulled her close to comfort her. Isabella looked at her husband. She was convinced Amber was telling the truth. She went to her husband. She expressed sympathy for Amber.

"Walt, we really need to do what we can to help them, dear."

Walter knew she was telling the truth partly because of the Delgado boy's reputation and the police report. He remembered an FBI agent on the case who had given an account of what happened. He wanted to help. He was just as worried as the rest of them.

"Don't worry, I'll figure something out. In the meantime, you probably need to get her to a more secure location. You had better contact your cousin because Ana wants her dead right away, and she knows exactly where she is. Everyone involved in the shoot-out is on her hit list, even the prosecuting attorney who failed to prosecute on behalf of her son and his crew. She feels enough time has passed and is ready for revenge."

"Dad, where do you suggest we take her?"

"Take her back to Little Rock, where we can keep an eye on her. I don't want her roaming around other states and getting into trouble. Son, wherever we take her, you will have to stay away in case Ana is still having you followed. I really don't trust her at this time. Stay here tonight, young lady, and I'll have someone come for you this weekend."

Amber looked puzzled. She looked at Santiago and then back at Walter and asked,

"Are you sure? Do you think we're going to be okay here?"

"If we were followed, I think it's best. You stay here." He reached behind him and took his weapon from its holster.

"You keep this tonight and if anyone so much as knocks on that door, you shoot through it."

"Okay, Mr. Burkett but I already have one."

"Take it anyway."

She took the weapon and placed it in a secure location out of Patrick Louis' reach. Santiago said, "Everything's going to be okay. If you have any problems, you call me okay."

"I will."

Santiago didn't want to leave. He looked back at her and whispered, "I love you." A tear fell from her cheek as he gently closed the door. She hurried and secured all the locks. She immediately called Cindy. Cindy was on stage performing when she called. As soon as she saw the missed call, she returned the call. Amber was sitting on the sofa. The ringing of the phone broke the silence in the room. Amber was spooked. She hurried and answered it so it wouldn't wake her son. "Cindy, I'm so glad you called."

"Is everything okay?"

"No, I just got word that Mrs. Delgado is going to have you killed."

"She's been threatening to kill me for a while. She hasn't done anything by now she's not going to, and besides, I've already told you I'm not running from her."

"No Cindy, that's just it. She's been waiting on purpose. She needed enough time to pass. Not only does she plan on killing you, but she wants all of your friends whose names are in the police report dead. That means Blaine and your friend Jessica and Big Dan, too."

Cindy was alarmed. Ana Maria was threatening to kill everyone she loved. She knew she was serious, and she wasn't going to stop until they were all dead. She was angry, and she wanted to go to her home and kill her herself. She was upset that she hadn't killed her along with her sons, but she felt that with

Anton and Andre dead, everything would be okay. Cindy planned to kill Anton anonymously, but he was always on the run. Then he had her delivered to his home where she killed him. If it wasn't for that, Ana Maria never would've known who killed her son.

"Amber, who told you this?"

"Santiago's father. They came by tonight, along with Santiago. They were concerned for his safety because Mrs. Delgado had him followed. She thought that you and I planned the deaths of the Delgado brothers, and it was done for the money. I told them the truth. I think they believed me."

"Perhaps so; I don't know who to trust now," Cindy admitted.

"Mr. Burkett gave me his weapon and told me to stay here tonight until he sends someone for us. What should I do? Do you think I can trust him?"

"I don't think so. I'm not sure. Let me call Jessica and Blaine to warn them. Also, I need to call Big Dan. We're going to come and get you ourselves. This could be a set-up. I don't trust anybody who works for that woman."

"Cindy if they wanted me dead, they would've already turned me over to her."

"So, what are you saying?"

"What is he waiting for? Why would Mr. Burkett give me his weapon? Does that sound like someone who is setting me up?"

"Amber, I can't think right now. What do you want me to do? Do you want me to come for you or not?"

"I think I'm going to wait it out."

"I think you need to let me help you. I don't want anything to happen to you or my little cousin. You may be a sitting duck."

"I'm okay I'm going to wait on Santiago."

Cindy didn't argue with her. She needed time to warn the others.

"Okay, Amber I have to go."

She called an urgent meeting with Jessica Barnes, Blaine, and Big Dan. Everyone met at her club. They went into her office. With worried expressions, they were curious as to why they were there. Cindy had already filled Blaine in on the situation. Jessica walked in dressed in all black. She had been on a case earlier. Her hair was in a ponytail. She was wearing her gun. Big Dan walked in looking like a one-man army. They gathered around, trying to find any available seat in her office. She closed the door behind them. "Okay, I just got word that Ana Maria Delgado has put a hit out on all of us. She's after everyone on the police report. I'm not about to sit by and let her hurt everyone I love, so what are we going to do? If the police kept her under surveillance twenty-four seven, she'd still remain a threat because she'll send someone else to do the job for her."

Jessica said, "Let's leak her plans to the media. We'll have them do an exclusive report on the issue; that way, she'll be on notice. If anything was to happen to either of us, she'd be suspected. It won't matter about the evidence. If so much as a hair on our heads is harmed, she'll look suspicious. That's all I got right now except for going right up to her and killing her."

Cindy had a wolfish expression on her face. She had killed before, and she would do it again. She didn't believe in sitting around waiting for trouble. She allowed everyone to come up with their own suggestions. Big Dan noticed the look in Cindy's eyes. They were of like mind. As far as they were concerned, killing Ana

Maria was the only way. He had a wife and five daughters. He was not about to take the threat lying down.

Once the meeting was over, the group immediately planned to report the threat to the authorities. Exposing her plot would be to their advantage.

They also decided to have the media run several stories simultaneously, as Jessica had suggested. They were on high alert. Ana Maria hadn't had a chance to pinpoint everyone, but she was sure that Walter would find them immediately, but he didn't. He'd been busy protecting his son.

CHAPTER EIGHT

Walter secured a place for Santiago and Amber. They were on a private road on a ten-acre spread in Lonoke County. They were far away from any neighbors, and the home was purchased in the name of one of Walter's businesses. They got settled in and were relaxing. In the meantime, Walter was at a meeting with Ana Maria and a few of her men about the hit list. She was ready to start tracking those she wanted to be killed. She wanted Walter's progress, but he couldn't show that he had been tracking her enemies. He was looking aloof. He sat staring into space thinking about Santiago.

"Burkett, did you hear me?" She asked, breaking his train of thought. "How is the search going?"

"I'm so sorry, Ana. I've been preoccupied with all these new cases you've added to my roster. I haven't had time for much of anything else, but I'm working on it. I'll have everyone tracked by the end of the week." She could tell something was bothering him.

"Is everything alright with Isabella?"

"Yes"

"What about Santiago?"

"He's fine too. I'll fill you in on that when we're alone."

"Okay, well, everyone, this meeting is adjourned. I need to speak with my brother in peace."

Ana Maria was truly concerned for her friends. If she loved you, then you knew you were loved, and she was very loyal. However, if she felt the slightest bit of mistrust or threat, she would turn on you and kill anyone she felt threatened by. Everyone finally exited the room. Once they were alone, she asked, "What's going on, Burkett?"

"It's Santiago. He's leaving for New York. He and his girlfriend have broken up. He's devastated and decided the move would be best for him. He says he wants to open his own law firm up there."

"So, our Santiago has a broken heart. He'll get over it. Perhaps we need to throw a party for him and invite a few lovely ladies. That should be a cure for any young man's broken heart."

"I don't think that will do it, at least not for him. You know, when he gets something in his head, it's there. His mother and I have talked and pleaded with him. His mind is made up. He's already left. We barely had a chance to say goodbye."

"How is Isabella taking the news?"

"About as well as any mother would. She understands it's his decision. Maybe he'll come around soon but for now, he's gone. I guess it's good for him to get away and clear his head."

Walter changed the subject. He looked at the list of names she'd given them. "I'm going to get on this today. Don't worry about a thing. You know I'll come through for you."

"You always do, Burkett." Walter left. He hoped she believed him. Now he had to begin tracking everyone on her list. He didn't necessarily want to. Santiago and Amber informed him that Big Dan, Blaine, and Jessica were all close to the family, and they didn't want them killed. The only other person left to track was the prosecuting attorney. He knew if he didn't deliver, Ana Maria would be disappointed. He didn't readily know what to do.

Isabella's feelings had changed towards her, and the bond she once shared was diminishing. She was slowly distancing herself from her best friend. She wanted to sever ties with her, but she didn't know how without her becoming suspicious. She couldn't believe how blind she had been during their friendship. Ana Maria helped her tremendously, but Isabella couldn't see how she allowed that to turn her into a subservient fool. She blindly followed her into every situation without question. She couldn't remember when she released her will over to her friend. It didn't happen all at once but over a period of years. She even allowed her to run her marriage, and she had more influence over Walter than she did. She was ready to change that for good. As she continued to distance herself, she noticed that Ana Maria would appear on her doorstep unannounced. It never bothered her before, but now she's totally annoyed by it. Isabella would do just enough to keep the conversation going, but she no longer felt indebted to her.

In their later years, Isabella and Walter had done far more for Ana than she had ever done for her in the beginning. She felt they were almost on an equal playing field, especially with all the killings, favors, and money they made her, but it wasn't like she was keeping score. She was very grateful to her friend. Ana Maria took the leading role by taking responsibility for Isabella and the rest of the women from Cuba. She knew what it was like to be abused in a time and place where no one really cared for them. She had suffered abuses at the hands of ruthless men. She wasn't built for abuse. She'd grown tough and begun to fight back. When she saw her helpless friends and the abuses they suffered at the hands of others, she took the teens under her wings and brought them into the Delgado organization. They, too, enjoyed the Delgado protection and a wonderful lifestyle to this day, with the exception of Rosalinda, whom the women killed.

Rosalinda wasn't as beautiful as the other girls, and she knew it. She was envious of her friends and, over the years, developed deep-seated hatred towards them. She watched for years as handsome men courted the other women, taking them on extravagant dates and fancy outings. Feeling left out, she became withdrawn and tried to keep to herself. Still, they continued caring for and including her in their circle. No one ever thought Ana Maria would actually kill Rosalinda, but she had gone too far, especially with all the kindness shown to her. Now Isabella couldn't help but think of that fateful day when they all killed their sister-friend.

If she could kill Rosalinda, she would kill not only her and Walter but Santiago as well, and Isabella knew it. She'd mourn their deaths afterwards, but she would definitely kill them. She felt a sense of betrayal that Ana Maria secretly followed her son, and she wasn't happy about it.

Jessica Barnes reported the death threats to the police. Because Jessica was a former police officer, she had connections in law enforcement. She also had a friend at the Federal Bureau of Investigations. Her name was agent Amy Stokes. She was actually on the case as an undercover agent when Cindy killed Anton Delgado. Her name was redacted from the police report, but her account of the events is what cleared Cindy and everyone else involved. Jessica informed her of the threat. Now that just about everyone from the Little Rock police department and the FBI knew about the hit list, Jessica's last call was to the media. She knew several journalists personally. After getting an okay from the station manager, they were allowed to work on the story. They prepared to run exclusive stories on the subject. The stories hit the press within one week with disclaimers, and the word alleged was thrown about, and hypothetical questions were posed to their own experts and audience. As the stories ran on the media circuit, all the targets laid low. The prosecuting attorney was in protective custody.

Ana Maria was finishing her dinner and preparing to eat her dessert when one of her loyal men came in and interrupted her. He was an elderly gentleman who had been with her for thirty-five years. He was her armed houseman, Raul.

"Madam Delgado"

"Yes, Raul, what is it?"

"I think you need to turn your television on. There's something on there that I believe you ought to see."

"But Raul, I'm enjoying this lovely music, and I'm about to eat my dessert. I'll watch it later."

"With all due respect, ma'am, I think you need to watch it now." The urgency of his voice and his facial expression told Ana Maria that she needed to do what he had requested.

"Get the remote and turn the television on," she said.

He did as he was told. She saw her face on the television screen. She was puzzled.

"Turn it up so I can hear it."

The male reporter was on the screen, and he began to speak,

"First on channel nine is the exclusive story of Ana Maria Delgado. Mrs. Delgado is rumored to be head of the Delgado crime family, whose alleged crimes can be dated as far back as the late sixties and early seventies. Her two sons were killed recently, only a few months apart. One was thought to be killed in retaliation for the murder of the leader of the Cassius White drug cartel. It happened at the Delgado estate in Miami. Cassius was rumored to have been murdered in what authorities are calling a drug deal gone wrong. Afterwards, a violent war ensued, and many people were killed in the Delgado Cartel. Apparently, the brothers went on the run and eventually made their way back to the state of Arkansas. According to a police report, Mrs. Delgado's son Anton kidnapped a couple of young ladies, one being his ex-girlfriend and the other her cousin. An undercover agent witnessed the incident and reported it. Others who knew the kidnapped women, aided in their rescue. The victims were forced to fight their way out of a fully armed compound filled with vicious criminals. On what must've been a horrific day, they barely escaped with their lives.

One of those witnesses told us in an exclusive interview that someone close to Ana Maria Delgado tipped them off, saying she's allegedly ordered everyone who was involved in the case to be killed. Due to the evidence at hand and witness testimony, no charges were brought against those protecting themselves against a ruthless criminal organization. The prosecuting attorney and his family are now in protective custody as well as the other potential targets. We have a special guest who's directly involved in the case, and she is giving us her account of what she learned. We've disguised her voice and her appearance so that she will remain anonymous." It was Jessica Barnes.

"We've learned there was a credible threat coming from an inside source that Ana Maria Delgado wants us dead. In the event this is found to be true, I've decided to come forth for the safety of all involved. The authorities are on notice, and everyone is under police protection at this time. If anything happens to either of these witnesses, we will assume it's because of Mrs. Delgado as no one else has a reason to harm these witnesses."

The reporter asked,

"Are you afraid for your life?"

"I'm afraid for the lives of my family and friends."

"I hear that she's looking for one young lady in particular who is rumored to have a grandchild she wants."

"I'm not at privy to discuss that, sir," Jessica said.

"I understand." He went on with Ana Maria's story and the family's history. Once the story was finished, he gave a disclaimer at the end.

"In the event that any of this is true, authorities aren't taking any chances because this family has long been suspected to be one of the most dangerous and ruthless in the state; still, the police have never been able to arrest or get a conviction on anyone within the organization. The Delgado name strikes fear in the hearts of many, and anyone found doing business with them mysteriously vanishes without a trace. At least for now, all these victims are accounted for, and the police are keeping a close watch on everyone, including Ana Maria Delgado."

Ana Maria was fuming while watching the story unfold. She knew someone close to her had leaked her plans. Only a few people actually knew about the list. She didn't know who to trust. She was angered. She called Walter and Isabella to see if they knew what was going on. She got no answer from them. They too, had watched the same newscast. They were alarmed. Walter said a little too much when speaking with Amber and Santiago. He was now upset because he knew Ana Maria would find that he was the leak.

They avoided her phone calls for the next two days. She had her driver take her to their home in the middle of the night. They pretended to be asleep and wouldn't come to the door. Isabella called her the following morning. She refused to meet with her face to face.

"Good morning."

"What do you mean, good morning? I've been trying to reach you and Walter for the past few days. What's going on with you?"

"Ana, we've been down ever since this thing with our son."

"I don't think so. I think it's more than that. I want to come over. I need to talk with you."

"I'm not feeling well." Ana Maria insisted on telling her what was on her mind.

"Somebody leaked my plans to the police and the media. My face has been plastered all over the airways because of it. I need Burkett to call me. After all, he is my attorney. They can't run a story like that. It's slanderous. I'm going to sue everyone who ran that story. Where in the hell is your husband?"

"I thought he was with you."

"No, I haven't seen him today."

"Well, try his cell phone."

"I've been calling him all morning. I've been calling both of you. I even stopped by there last night. Neither of you would come to the door."

"I took a sleeping pill. I needed the rest. My nerves have been on edge lately."

"You've never ignored my calls; neither has Burkett. Hell, I even called Santiago, and he's not answering my calls." Puzzled as to why she was calling her son, Isabella asked,

"What do you need with Santiago?"

"I called him to see if he had heard from you."

Isabella was quiet. She waited to see what Ana Maria would say next. She heard the phone go dead. She knew she was upset with her. Ana Maria was thinking about Isabella. *"When I told her about the news story, she didn't comment on it. Something's not right."* She called Raul into the room.

"Yes, Madam Delgado."

"Have Luis get the car. I have some errands to run."

"Yes ma'am."

She went to Isabella's home, relaxed in the back seat, and watched the house. "Luis, I'm going to knock on the door. While I'm inside, I need you to place a tracking device on her car."

"Yes, Ma'am."

They pulled into the huge driveway. She got out and rang the doorbell. Isabella looked out of the peephole but refused to open the door. While she was at the door, Luis placed the tracker on her car. He quickly got back in the vehicle. Ana Maria spat at the door as a sign of disgust with Isabella. She got into the back seat of her vehicle. They waited around the block. After about an hour and a half, Isabella exited the house and got in her car. She drove for about forty minutes outside of town. She pulled up to the home where Santiago and Amber were staying. She didn't notice the vehicle following her. Luis didn't pull into the long driveway. Ana Maria got her binoculars and watched the house from the road. She could see Santiago. Isabella went inside and stayed there for an hour. Ana Maria's car drove away. She would come back later. She called Walter from inside the vehicle. She still got no answer.

Over the next few nights, she watched the Burketts going to Santiago's place. She finally got a call from Walter. As he continued giving her excuse after excuse for not contacting her, she listened, knowing he was lying to her. She interrupted him and asked, "How is Santiago doing?"

"He's doing okay, but he's still broken-hearted."

"Oh, how's he getting along in New York?"

"He's making it just fine."

"That's good to know. I'm glad he's doing okay."

120

She instantly knew that Walter was the one responsible for the authorities learning of the list.

"I need to speak with you about the story the media is reporting about me concerning the list. Do you know how they learned of it? How can they report that type of information? Aren't they liable for reporting information that slanders me? Or is it all a part of your plan to set me up?" Walter exhaled.

"I've never tried to set you up. I didn't tell the police about the list. Remember, if you go down, so do I. So why would I say anything?" Unconvinced, she said,

"You're acting unusually suspicious, and you and Isabella won't take my calls. You won't answer the door for me, and I haven't heard from you in a few days. You both keep telling me it's about Santiago, but I would like to know the real truth. I've heard from the rest of my men. They aren't dodging me. They've been here with me the entire time. The only people who've changed are you and Isabella."

"I told you we've been very busy. What do you need me to do for you today?"

"I want you to look into the media's accusation about the list. Check into it and tell me my rights. I will sue every station who ran that piece of garbage."

"I'll check into it further. I have to go now; I have court."

"Alright."

After ending his call with Ana Maria, Walter called his wife and asked her to stay away from her until further notice. Isabella had no plans to see her anyway. After talking to her husband, she made a few more phone calls. She got dressed and got her keys so she could go and see her son. She opened the entry door and tried to leave. The blood immediately drained from her face. With widened eyes, her heart sank. She was frozen with fear when she realized her pathway was being blocked by Ana Maria.

"Going somewhere, my friend?" Ana Maria asked, forcing her back inside at gunpoint.

CHAPTER NINE

Cindy and Blaine were having dinner. Two police officers were placed outside her home around the clock for protection. She refused to go into hiding. Blaine, a former LRPD officer, knew the officers on duty. One was a friend named Lieutenant Gary Fitz. Blaine worked under him when he was on the force. He volunteered for the job because he and Blaine were good friends. After dinner, Blaine stepped outside to speak with Lt. Fitz.

"So, I see you've pissed off the *big* She-Devil!" Lt. Fitz said. His tall thin frame stood firm while his hand rested on his service weapon.

"Everybody pisses her off. She hates everyone. She's the type to kill and eat her own young. She never knows when to quit. I'm surprised the feds have never made anything stick on her or her men," said Blaine.

"She's probably going senile up in that big ass compound all by herself."

"She's not by herself. She has what amounts to a small army up there with her. Not to mention everyone she owns in this state. She thrives on power and control. She uses people as tools to do her dirty work."

"So, what's this I hear of her having a grandchild?" Lt. Fitz asked.

"You know how it goes. She wants to get her hands on the baby, but Cindy isn't having it. Can you believe she wants to kill the girl just so she can take the baby and raise him to take over the family business?" Lt. Fitz asked,

"So is the girl hidden in a safe location?"

"Yes, her and her boyfriend."

"She has a boyfriend huh?"

"Yes. He was hired to find her and take her to Mrs. Delgado, but he hid her instead. I don't know where they are. They keep us out of that, but as long as they're safe, it's good."

"How do you know they're safe? How do you know she hasn't already harmed them?"

"I know because we talk to them daily."

"When is the last time you heard from them?" Lt. Fitz asked.

"Cindy talked to her last night. Why do you ask?"

"I'm just curious. I want to make sure everyone is okay. You know how much I care about you and Cindy. So, how are Sheila and the boys?" Lt. Fitz asked, speaking of Blaine's ex-wife and children.

"They're doing okay under the circumstances. Sheila feels like her privacy is being violated but she knows having the officers there is necessary for their safety."

"Yeah, I know it's a bummer to have to bring them into this, but for everyone's safety it's necessary."

They continued talking for a while until Cindy called Blaine inside to help her move a piece of furniture.

"I gotta go, Lt. Cindy needs my help."

Lt. Fitz looked inside and saw Cindy trying to move a large desk around. She was moving it away from the window. He offered to help. They all began to move the desk together. Cindy's burner cell phone rang.

"That's Amber, I have to get that?" she said to Blaine. They took a brief break while Cindy answered her phone. "Come on Lt. We can move this without her." Lt. Fitz was preoccupied. He tried to listen in on Cindy's phone call, but she continued the call in another room. "Lieutenant," Blaine said out loud, which startled him. "Pick up your end, and let's move it over here. I think this is where she wants it."

He continued to help Blaine move the table. He tried listening again, but he couldn't hear anything.

After being on the call for about ten minutes, she finally came back into the room.

"Is everything okay, Cindy?" Blaine asked, concerned.

"Yes, she and Santiago are on the move. They see a suspicious car outside of their home."

"What are they going to do?" Blaine asked.

"Blaine, I need to run a quick errand. I'll be right back."

"Babe, is everything okay?"

"Yeah."

"It's too dangerous for you to be out there alone. Let me go with you," said Blaine. Lt. Fitz stepped towards Cindy, trying to deter her from leaving.

"Cindy, you know I'll get into trouble if I allow you to leave alone and something were to happen to you. My orders are to guard you at all times and not allow you to leave my sight. You need to let me escort you, at least."

"I'll be okay," she said, grabbing her bag and throwing it over her shoulder. She ran out of the door. Lt. Fitz called ahead to tell his captain about Cindy leaving without cover. He looked at Blaine and asked,

"Are you just going to let her leave like that?"

"When she has her mind made up, there's no stopping her. You'd be better off stopping a Brahma bull with your bare hands." Blaine walked off. Lt. Fitz made a few personal calls and went back to hanging out until his shift was over.

Sisters Til Death Parts Us.

Isabella was sitting on her sofa after a forceful push by Ana Maria who was standing over her.

"Mi Hermana, we need to talk." Isabella, simmering with anger, asked, "What is it, Ana?"

"It's wonderful how you pretend you don't know. I can't believe you and your family would betray me after all I've done for you. I thought you and I were sisters. I thought you, of all people, loved me. How could you turn on me?"

"What are you talking about?" I've never turned on you. I love you. You know that."

"Oh, so you love me. If you love me, then tell me why you and your family are consorting with my enemies?"

"What do you mean?" Ana Maria was still standing over her.

"Hermana, stop pretending that you don't know what I'm talking about," she said to Isabella.

"Please tell me what you're referring to."

Alright, I'm going to pretend you don't know. Allow me to fill you in on the details. I've discovered that your family's been assisting my son's killer and her family. Santiago has been hiding my grandson for some time now. He's managed to keep this from me while still handling my business and eating at my home. What have I done to deserve this treatment? You and Walter aided your son in a plot to hide my grandson from me. If that's not bad enough, Walter leaks my plans, and the media runs a story about it. You know I don't like my business in the streets."

Isabella's nerves were on edge. Fear snaked through her body,

"Let me explain,"

"Ahhh…your memory is back. Okay, let me hear what you have to say, sister."

"I demanded that Santiago bring the girl to us. You know the boy isn't like us. He has a soft heart. He was concerned that you were going to hurt the girl. When I found out what my son had done, I was upset with him. I wanted you to have your grandchild, but I knew you wouldn't forgive Santiago for what he'd done. You would've had him killed. I couldn't take that chance. It was my duty to protect my son. He was very close to your boys, and he felt he was honoring Andre by allowing his son to have a chance at a normal life." Ana Maria interrupted her,

"It's not his place to make that decision about my blood. That's for me to decide."

"You may be right, but what rights does the mother have? You're talking about your rights, but what about the child? Doesn't he have the right to a loving mother? Every child needs their mother especially since his father is dead. You're well up in age so if you kill the mother and something were to happen to you, who would be left to take care of the child? You never think these things through. You simply make rash decisions without regard for the consequences. Santiago loves your grandchild. He wants a better life for him."

"I can give him a better life!"

"No, you can't; the only things you can provide for him are material. You will introduce him to a life of crime that is filled with pain and misery. What if he follows in your footsteps and ends up in the organization? What if he goes to prison for life or worse, would end up like your sons? Is that what you want for him?"

"Whatever I want for him, it's my decision to make; not you and your family. Santiago has taken it upon himself to raise my grandson. To me, that is the ultimate betrayal. I have no family. That child is my last hope at seeing the Delgado name carried on."

"Ana, he will always be a Delgado, and the name will go on. That'll never change. Why can't you just let this go and leave him a healthy legacy instead of a destructive lifestyle? You should retire, and then you could have your grandson on your lap every evening if you so choose, but you refuse to give up this lifestyle."

Ana Maria, still fuming with anger and contempt said,

"You weren't complaining when my lifestyle saved your ass. You weren't complaining when I took a bullet for you or when you were benefiting from my life of crime. You're no better than me. We're the same. You've killed just as many men and committed just as many crimes as I have."

"Yes Ana, but I know when to quit. Enough is enough. We've killed all our enemies. We're old now. It's time to put down the guns and pick up our grandchildren."

"Isabella, you have your son. I've lost both of mine. Your son is the only thing keeping me from my kin. Since he has taken it upon himself to make me his enemy, he must die."

"I love you, Ana. We didn't set out to betray you. I only wanted to protect my child. I love you both, but how could you ask me to choose between you and my son? A loving mother will choose her children, and you would do the same. I'm not going to sit by and allow you to kill my child."

"It's not about whether or not you're going to allow me to kill him. It's going to happen. Maybe then you'll understand the pain I felt of losing my sons, and perhaps you'll stop interfering in my life. He not only betrayed me, but he betrayed my son by helping his killers escape the punishment they deserve. My sons died the Delgado way; they never wavered, and they stayed right by my side until their deaths. They died with honor. Killing Santiago would bring honor to my sons."

"There is no honor in dead children, Ana."

"That's a matter of perspective, but you'll soon know my pain, my beautiful sister. I want you to know that I've found your son. My men are with him right now. I'm having him and the girl delivered to me."

Hearing the news of her son's capture, heated rage swept over her. Isabella violently stood to her feet. She pushed Ana Maria with her chest. Grimacing, Ana Maria stepped backward as Isabella got square in her face.

"Ana, this is a new low, even for you. You'd better not lay a hand on my boy do you hear me?"

"I'm going to do what I said. Don't worry, I won't kill you, but I will kill Walter; I mean it's only right. After all, I killed my husband to protect all of us. With no husband or child, you'll know my pain. Perhaps you'll have the rest of your life to think of how horrible it feels to live without your son, and you're completely helpless to do anything about it. I'm going to make you regret turning your back on me. You know the old saying goes; you don't bite the hand that feeds you. I'm going to make sure you die broke. You don't deserve a damn thing. Everything you and Walter have is because of me. You were able to send your son to those fancy schools. He was getting the best education and living a lavished and pampered life, while it was me and my sons who got our hands dirty to keep this organization going."

"You're wrong, Ana. It's the other way around. Walter and I have been right here with you. It's because of Walter's connections that you still have this organization. Your empire had all but crumbled until Walter and I helped you build it back up. You and your men were on your way to prison until Walter and his friends made all those little investigations into your organization disappear. They had so much evidence on all of us, and you know it. We'd still be rotting away in prison if it weren't for Walter.

Yes, you took care of me in the beginning, but I have long since paid my dues, and as far as my son's education is concerned, yes, I chose better for him. You could've done the same with your children. You chose their life for them. They had other goals and dreams. Your sons turned out just how you wanted them to, yet you blame me? You have no one to blame but yourself."

While they were talking, there was a knock at the door. It was Ana Maria's hired assassins. Isabella watched as several of her armed gunmen marched Santiago, Amber, Cindy, Jessica Barnes, Big Dan, and Blaine into her living room. The leader was Lieutenant Gary Fitz, who was not only friends with Blaine and Jessica but also trusted by the city's police department to protect them. He was on Ana Maria's payroll, among other officials.

"Well, look who decided to join us. Come on in and join the party. It all ends here for you. You'll die tonight right here in the home of my number one enemy. I'm going kill you and burn this godforsaken building to the ground. The smoke of your burning carcasses will fill the heavens," Ana Maria said while each of her enemies marched into Isabella's place at gunpoint.

Isabella was upset when she saw her Santiago being paraded around like a criminal. Amber looked around in horror, as did the other captives. Amber had her arms wrapped tightly around her son. She refused to let him go until one of Ana Maria's female workers ripped him from her arms. She took the screaming child to Ana Maria, who instantly fell in love with him.

She tried to reach for him, but he refused to go to her. She held him anyway, but he began violently kicking and fighting her while screaming for his mother, further fueling Ana Maria's anger.

She felt that the child was acting out because he wasn't allowed in her life early on. She tried to calm him, but her attempts were unsuccessful. He continued screaming at the top of his lungs at the sight of her. Amber tried calming him,

"Patrick, mommy's here." The worker tried to take him to his mother. Ana Maria yelled,

"Don't take him to her; get him out of here. I don't want him to ever see her fucking face again."

The lady did as she was told and took him away. Ana Maria walked up to Santiago, who was being detained by two men. "Do you see what you've done to me? You have managed to keep my grandson away from me so long that he hates me."

She slapped him hard in the face. Then she spat at his feet.

"You're a fucking disgrace, a fucking uppity ingrate. You and your parents took advantage of my love for you. You've turned on me, siding with my enemies. You were like a son to me. I made you homemade meals with my very own hands. I made your parents rich so they could afford you the lifestyle you've become accustomed to. The private schools and your lavish life were all because of me. What do you have to say for yourself?"

Santiago's clothing and hair was disheveled due to Ana Maria's henchmen roughing him up. His face was worn with worry, and he was concerned for all involved. His deep blue eyes were filled with contempt. Holding back his anger, he drew in a deep breath and said,

"With all due respect, Mrs. Delgado, I did this in honor of Andre. Neither of your sons wanted to be a part of this organization. They longed to live a better life. They expressed their true feelings to me early on and they begged me not to get involved with the family business. They were forced into it, and they hated it."

She slapped him again.

"How dare you lie on my boys?" Not caring about the slap to his face, he shifted his eyes towards his mother, then to Amber, and then back to Ana Maria.

"You can assault me all you want, but that won't change the truth. They hated this organization. They wanted to live normal lives, but you were so obsessed with the business that you lost sight of what was really important. Anton confided in me. He had other goals and dreams, and so did Andre. Did you know that Anton secretly got his college degree but failed to mention it to you? He worked hard for it. He wanted to see if he had what it took to survive without being attached to the underworld. He was working on his doctorate, but he died before he could complete it. It was something he needed to do as a form of therapy from all the killing, other criminal activities, and the mind control you had over him. There were many accomplishments you were unaware of because they feared you wouldn't support their dreams. You treated them like you were their handlers. You owned them. They were afraid of you just like everyone else."

Her mood plummeted as he revealed the truth about her children. Hearing his account of her sons caused a great weight to settle on her heart. She became unglued. She wanted to know more, but she had an audience and a room full of enemies that were witnessing just how poor of a mother she had been to her kids. She tried to remain strong and in control of the situation. She ordered Santiago to be quiet. Her heart couldn't take much more. She knew he was telling the truth. The sharp truth stabbed her through the heart like a dagger. He was now ready to twist it as he began to reveal more truths.

"Here's something else you don't know. That child in there is not your only grandchild." She could barely believe what she was hearing. "What the fuck are you talking about, little Burkett?

"As I said, that's not the only grandchild you have. You actually have four granddaughters and three more grandsons, all of whom belong to Anton. They're very beautiful children. Care to know where they are and their ages? Well, I know them very well, and I also know that Anton wanted to keep them away from you. That's probably why he never mentioned this baby to you. It was his way of protecting his own nephew from you. I mistakenly told you because I thought you may have already known. Imagine my surprise when I realized you didn't. I hate that I told you. Yes, Anton tried to protect his seed from this lifestyle. They were at his memorial service but under my protection. You'll never know who they are. I'm honored to go to my grave with his secret, especially since I know we're all going to die here today. I had papers drawn up that in the event of Amber's death, you'll never get custody of that child. It doesn't matter who you kill; you have no legal rights to him, so go ahead and do what you do best. We're going to die together as friends and family, but you'll die a lonely, miserable old bitty. You'll have the pleasure of knowing that not only did your kids abhor you, but your grandchildren will be told about your evil deeds, and they will hate you, too. You're angry with me for not being loyal to you, and you're right. I may not have been loyal to you, but I was loyal to your sons, and I kept their secrets because they were truly my friends. Now, who really loved them more, me or you? You forced them against their will. I honored them by keeping my promise to them."

Ana began to shake her head violently. She gripped her forehead while gritting her teeth as she heard voices in her mind. The voices were of her sons and grandchildren laughing and shunning her. She couldn't believe what her sons had done to her. It was disturbing to hear that they'd actually shut her grandchildren

134

out of her life. She yelled for someone to fix her a drink. After one was handed to her, she began to down the elixir to drown the voices. After a few minutes of calm, she asked herself, *"Is he telling me the truth?"* She knew in her gut that he was being truthful. Her eyes filled with tears as sadness overtook her. She was embarrassed by the way Santiago was speaking to her. She wanted to plead with him for more information. The news of having more grandchildren was almost more than she could bear. At that moment, she wanted mercy.

"Please son, tell me about them. I'll spare your life if you do."

"Mrs. Delgado, I can't, and I won't."

"Santiago, I thought you loved me?"

"You make it hard for people to love you by your actions. I care about you, and I've grown to love and respect you, but I hate your evil ways. You only love me because of who my parents are, yet here we stand today, about to die at your hands because we have chosen to protect your sons' children. As far as your love goes, that's a very thin line with you. You have no mercy, and you're ruthless. Nobody loves you but my parents. Everyone else is simply afraid of you. Let that sink in when you're awake at night wondering why your own son didn't want you around his kids. I'll gladly lay my life on the line if it means you'll never get your hands on them."

Lt. Fitz stepped forward and asked, "Ma'am, what do you want me to do with them?"

"Line them up. We're going down to her basement. Once there, I'll kill them all and burn this place to the ground, but first, we'll wait until her husband comes home."

Everyone was escorted into the basement. A flood of emotions overtook her. She went to Isabella's bar and fixed herself another drink. She sat on a bar stool, thinking about everything Santiago told her. She wished she had the heart to kill him at that moment, but she couldn't find the strength. She was more curious about the grandchildren she'd never met. She knew that once he died, the hopes of her ever knowing who her grandchildren were would die with him. She was devastated to learn that Anton had kept his children away from her. She tried to imagine what they must look like. In a burst of anger and confusion, she threw the glass against the wall and began to sob.

She couldn't run the risk of her men seeing her cry, so she went into the restroom. She whispered a cry, *"Anton, my son, why did you do this to me?"* She briefly tried to replay the last forty years of her life and how her own sons had come to mistrust her. They showed no signs of hatred, only loyalty, but she had gotten fear confused with loyalty and love with acceptance. She realized at that moment, that her sons served her out of duty. She was confused. She felt the world had turned against her. She talked to herself,

"Why does everyone I love hate me? Why have they all turned on me after all I've done for them? My husband and sons, my best friends, all hated me. Nobody really loved me."

She began to sink back into the old feelings of abandonment. The despair and hopelessness she felt brought back memories of how it was when her parents were killed. As a young girl on the streets of Cuba, she had been attacked and sexually assaulted many times. She learned how to survive by gaining the mental strength she needed to carry on. She knew how ruthless and cold-hearted men could be towards a young woman on the streets.

She vowed that she would never allow another person to abuse her or rape her, so she began to fight back. As the years passed, she grew colder and more evil than ever. Because of all the pain she endured, she found it difficult to trust anyone, and the more successful she became, the more people seemed to hate her. Once she recognized her adversaries, she would kill them, take over their businesses, and move on to the next victim, gaining her the reputation of the most evil and shrewd woman alive.

Everyone, knowing her capabilities, complied out of fear. It just wasn't worth the battle going against her, especially after witnessing how she managed to destroy the lives of so many innocent people and was never charged.

After washing and drying her face, she walked out of the bathroom feeling defeated. She knew she had a difficult task at hand. She was about to kill everyone she loved: Santiago, Isabella, and Walter. Once they were dead, she would be alone. She was losing the thirst for their blood, and she knew it wasn't going to be as rewarding as she'd hoped, but she would kill them.

She thought of committing a murder-suicide, but she was too full of pride to end her own life. She slowly walked into the living room where Luis was patiently waiting for her.

Walter walked in the front door. He looked at Ana Maria and Luis standing in his living room.

"Hello Ana, what are you doing here?"

"Come on in, Burkett. We have something to discuss." He walked in but left his entry door ajar.

"Where's Isabella?"

Ana Maria looked at him, wanting to cry but trying to hold her composure.

"Isabella is downstairs along with Santiago and the girl."

"What the fuck did you do, Ana?"

"Nothing yet; we were waiting for you to join the party," she said still trying to prove she was in control. Luis stood firm with his weapon in his hand. He motioned for Walter to go ahead of them to the basement. When she reached the bottom of the dark stairway, her eyes briefly scanned the basement. That's when she noticed all her men had been subdued, and her captives were no longer under the gun. She'd been set up. Lt. Fitz was in position with his weapon aimed at Ana Maria and Luis. Blaine and Jessica Barnes were armed, and they stood guarding her and Luis from the side. Cindy and Big Dan were a little farther in the distance, guarding Ana Maria's henchmen to ensure they wouldn't escape. Amber and Santiago hid in an adjacent room, hoping the plan worked. Isabella was also in the room but was unaware of the plan to trap Ana Maria and her men.

As instructed by Lt. Fitz, Walter left the entry door open for his officers to enter. They waited for the signal that Ana Maria and her guys had been subdued. Lt. Fitz aimed his weapon towards Luis, who was still armed.

"Drop your weapon, Luis!" Luis aimed his weapon towards Walter because he was in the direct line of fire. He fired off a round, nicking Walter in the right shoulder and causing him to kneel in pain. Lt. Fitz responded by firing on Luis, shooting him in the heart. He was dead before he hit the basement floor. Ana Maria lifted her gun and began firing at Lt. Fitz, but he struck her in the chest several times, fatally wounding her. Lt. Fitz gave the all-clear signal. Isabella, Amber, and Santiago came from their hiding place, relieved the ordeal was over. Isabella quickly tended to her husband.

"I'm okay, darling. It's just a small scratch," he said, kissing his wife. Isabella looked behind her husband and noticed Ana Maria lying on the floor with blood droplets coming from her nose and mouth. Her body had landed face down when the bullets hit her. Her left hand rested underneath her body, while her right hand was barely hanging on to her prized pistol. She was dead long before this moment. Her dead eyes, which stared downward, seemed to match her previous life. It only took a few bullets from the Lieutenant's gun to complete death's mission.

Seeing her friend's lifeless body lying on the floor, Isabella ran to her side, fell to her knees, and let out a loud cry. She took her right hand and gently closed her eyes, saying a brief prayer over her.

"I love you, Mi Hermosa Hermana," she said, gently sobbing. Although she was hurting over her friend's death, she was relieved the ordeal was over.

Ana Maria was pronounced dead at the scene, and her men were taken into custody.

To gain access to the inside of Ana Maria's inner circle, Lt. Fitz befriended one of her corrupt workers within the police department. His superiors recruited him, playing the role of a corrupt cop infiltrating the Delgado operation. He was ordered to watch over those targeted by her so he could learn of her plans. After being ordered to bring her enemies in for execution, Lt. Fitz had his own plan. Each victim who was escorted into Isabella's home at gunpoint was heavily armed and wearing body armor.

Ana Maria's men were in for a fight and didn't know it. The group had devised the plan hoping to provoke a gun battle, with the end goal resulting in Ana's death. As long as she was alive, everyone's lives would be in danger, and they knew it.

They knew she would never kill the baby. Amber, who was tired of running, agreed to be a target. She, too, was armed in the event something went wrong. Walter played his role as well. Lt. Fitz had a few officers who were friends on standby.

He didn't inform his superiors of his plan. He knew his plan wouldn't meet their approval. If they discovered what he'd done, he would lose his job and possibly face prosecution. His friendship with Blaine and Jessica was a major factor in his putting not only his career in jeopardy but also his life. He was confident that he could accomplish the mission with very little manpower, and since Jessica and Blaine had experience in law enforcement, it was the best course of action for all involved. Ana Maria Delgado was finally dead after decades as a career criminal. She had an elaborate funeral fit for royalty, and her body was laid to rest in Cuba. The remaining members of Los Zorros Blancos, including Isabella, were in attendance. Ultimately, her money was left to Isabella, and as Ana Maria's attorney, Santiago helped administer the will to his mother's estate.

He set up trusts for each of Anton's children and finally gave Amber the money that Andre set aside for Patrick Louis. He also contacted several people he knew personally who'd been scammed by Ana Maria. He released their property and funds back to the rightful owners who were affected by her. He was doing his best to right her wrongs. His mother sought to make restitution for her crimes.

She and Walter turned their backs on the life of crime and went straight, hoping the feds would never find out about their crimes in the Delgado cartel. With Ana Maria dead, the empire crumbled. Those who had formerly worked for her went their separate ways. They were free to live normal lives. They weren't as loyal as she'd thought; they, too, served her out of fear.

Santiago and Amber purchased a large home in New York City. He opened one of the largest and most successful law firms, which had been his goal all along. Amber finally got her law degree, and she worked alongside Santiago. She also followed her dreams of becoming an actress and worked in small films and a few shows on Broadway. After realizing her dream of acting, she and Santiago were married in a small ceremony at her parents' home in Arkansas.

Her parents could finally relax from their life on the run and enjoy their retirement. Amber's father fished daily from one of the two boats she purchased for him, with her mother right by his side. Santiago officially adopted Patrick Louis, who is now a Burkett.

Cindy and Blaine settled back into their normal routine. They were settled in for a cozy evening. They ordered take-out. After paying the delivery guy, Cindy walked into the living room, where Blaine watched the news. A clip about the Delgados was being aired. Cindy looked at Blaine and said,

"Baby, turn the TV off. The one name I don't ever want to hear again in my life is Delgado." Blaine took the remote and turned the TV off, tossing it across the room.

"Thanks, babe," she said, planting a kiss on his lips. "Babe, life with you has proven to be quite an adventure. I wonder what it is about us that always causes trouble to find us, from murderous exes, evil grandmothers, serial killers, and other criminals. It's a wonder we're still alive."

Blaine chuckled, "Hey, I never promised you that living with me would be easy."

"It's been quite an adventure, a real roller coaster ride for sure," said Cindy.

"Well, look on the bright side; at least you'll never get bored," said Blaine.

They kissed.

About The Author

Karen Coleman is an Arkansas native. She enjoys writing exciting and dramatic stories. A phenomenal author with a distinctive style, she has demonstrated a sensational talent for steering her readers through every line and page with eager anticipation.

Karen has published several novels in various genres. Readers have described her novels as riveting, fast-paced, and thrilling.

Her teen novels are insightful and empowering. As a mentor who has worked with teens for many years, Karen understands the social challenges they face, and she skillfully addresses those topics with a finesse that lends excitement, adventure, and encouragement.

A self-proclaimed fiction writer with an element of truth, Karen began penning her thoughts as a hobby. After many years of writing and encouragement from those around her, she began writing more intensely, eventually turning out several wonderful novels. She offers something for almost every reader. There's something to enjoy from her adult crime series to her teen books. Her literary works have garnered much fanfare and have not only been enjoyed by her many readers; she's highly celebrated among her writing peers. Her books are meant to inspire, uplift, and entertain, leaving her audience asking for more.

Karen is also a playwright, actor, and former city council member. She's the mother of four and a Glam-ma of thirteen and counting. Her grandchildren affectionately call her Nana. She's also the proud mom of two rambunctious miniature schnauzers. She spends time crafting, fishing, or enjoying a great barbecue when not writing or spoiling her grandbabies.

OTHER BOOKS BY THE AUTHOR

Arkansas Heat "A City Scorned"

Arkansas Heat "A Brutha's Obsession"

Arkansas Heat "Cindy's Revenge"

Arkansas Heat "Raising Delgado"

Arkansas Heat "Deceptive Practices"

Closer Than Enemies 1& 2

Frozen Dreams

In the Wrong Game

Metamorphosis "Good Girl Gone Bad"

Morgan's Path

No Place for Emily Ann

Whatever Happened to I Love You?

I Am a Whole Being, Finding Wholeness after Rejection, Abandonment, Pain & Loss

I Am a Whole Being Activity Journals and Coloring books.